G.I.JOE
THE RISE OF COBRA

Also from Titan Books

G.I. JOE: Above and Beyond
by Max Allan Collins

THE RISE OF COBRA

Max Allan Collins

Story by Michael Gordon and Stuart Beattie
and Stephen Sommers

Screenplay by Stuart Beattie and David Elliot
and Paul Lovett

Based on Hasbro's G.I Joe' Characters

TITAN BOOKS

G.I. Joe: The Rise of Cobra
ISBN: 9781848564084

Published by
Titan Books
A division of
Titan Publishing Group Ltd.
144 Southwark St
London
SE1 0UP

First edition June 2009.

10 9 8 7 6 5 4 3 2 1

G.I. Joe: The Rise of Cobra is a work of fiction. Names, characters, places, and incidents
are the products of the author's imagination or are used fictitiously. Any resemblance
to actual events, locales, or persons, living or dead, is entirely coincidental.

Visit our websites:
www.titanbooks.com
www.hasbro.com

Did you enjoy this book? We love to hear from our readers. Please email us at
readerfeedback@titanemail.com or write to us at Reader Feedback at the above address.

To receive advance information, news, competitions, and exclusive Titan offers online,
please register as a member by clicking the "sign up" button on our website:
www.titanbooks.com

A CIP catalogue record for this title is available from the British Library.

Printed and bound in Great Britain by CPI Group UK Ltd.

In memory of
Marine Corporal Jon McRae

A TIP OF THE HELMET

I would like to thank Michael Kelly of Hasbro, Inc., for his stellar support; writing a novel based on the screenplay of a major picture, particularly an action-oriented one like *G.I. JOE: The Rise of Cobra,* would be almost impossible without access to set photos, cast lists, and costume reference, all of which Michael provided, sometimes within minutes of a research request.

Also, I would like to thank and credit screenwriters Stuart Beattie and Skip Woods for their lively screenplay, as well as director Stephen Sommers, whose *Mummy* franchise I have been fortunate to serve with four prior movie novels.

Thank you, too, to a number of folks at Del Rey Books, from Scott Shannon and Keith Clayton, who first got me involved with the project at the 2007 San Diego Comic Con, to editors Tricia Narwani, Susan Moe, and Betsy Mitchell, who provided guidance, advice, and support.

Also, a nod to my associate Matthew Clemens, who gathered background material (from comics to animation) to help bring someone who did not grow up with the G.I. JOE universe properly up to speed.

Finally, I would encourage readers who enjoyed this novel to seek out its prequel, *G.I. JOE: Above and Beyond*.

Prologue:

Paris, 1641
The Bastille

The moon could not break through the cold, misty fog that swirled around the imposing walls of the Bastille like smoke from the aftermath of some great conflagration. Tens of thousands of bricks comprised the eight-towered fortress/prison at Number 232, rue Saint-Antoine, an imposing structure surrounded by a broad moat and resembling nothing so much as a hellish castle.

Within these walls were every variety of criminal imaginable, from rapist to murderer, from swindler to thief; but many here were religious prisoners, guilty of the crime of writing down and publishing their beliefs. Some cells were home to high-ranking political prisoners and these accommodations could be as pleasant as the several residential buildings within the walls.

But the majority of the cells were as wretched as anything the worst prisons in Paris could provide. Testimony to this fact were the screams echoing across the snow-covered courtyard from barred windows, wails of agony indicating despair here, torture there, and none of it seemed to penetrate the stolid resolve of the prison guards on patrol with their pikes in hand, outside.

Inside, along a row of filthy, foul-smelling cells strode two prison guards in dark, dingy doublets who were also oblivious to the suffering of the whimpering, starving prisoners, who were like pale ghosts in the flicker of wall-mounted torches. The big black rat in one corner, nibbling a stray crust of bread, showed more interest in the passing guards than those guards displayed for their charges.

Yet when the guards came to a stop at a particular cell, its inhabitant was not among the whimpering nor, for that matter, the starving. He was a big man whose trousers and blouse showed the dirt and rips of abuse, but whose quietly defiant countenance—a strong narrow face dominated by high cheekbones and hooded blue eyes—indicated neither fear nor defeat.

James McCullen had been allowed the privilege of retaining a certain red square medallion around his neck, the symbol of the Scotsman's clan. Perhaps his captors had hoped he would try to harm himself with it. Or perhaps none of them had wished to find out what might happen should they try to remove it. . . .

His smile was mocking, his eyes glaring.

"Going for a wee walk, are we, lads?" the prisoner asked. "Bonny night for it. Come on in and enjoy the view from my palace window."

The guard nearest the bars sneered and snarled, "On your feet, ye Scottish pig."

"How can I resist so gracious an invitation?"

Keys clanked as did the prisoner's shackles, and then the two towering guards were leading their muscular prisoner down dank hallways; such processions were uncommon here, as the captives were seldom let out of their cages, though on those rare occasions, the reason was never a pleasant one.

Soon McCullen was being led by the guards across the courtyard, boots crunching ice-frosted snow. The crisp air, the mist that had little icy teeth in it, felt good to the prisoner. He sucked that air in, and he relished the cold. He had not been outside in some time, and suspected he might never again have that opportunity.

The heat of the furnace room that met McCullen quickly replaced the cold, this new temperature nothing the prisoner might relish, not when he could see the two massive prison workers in leather aprons, in the process of molding something in the open fiery maw of the furnace, maneuvering a huge chunk of molten metal in red-hot tongs.

Bare-chested now, McCullen was forced by the guards into a waiting, standing rack. A robed priest stood solemnly if mercilessly nearby, reciting the Lord's Prayer in Latin. The warden, in dark doublet, hose, and breeches, was nearby as well, also reading, but in French.

"James McCullen," the plump, mustachioed warden said, eyes on the scroll of paper he held pompously before him, "you have been found guilty of treason for the sale of military arms to the enemies of our Lord, King Louis XIII. . . ."

McCullen said nothing. The charges were, after all, quite true.

". . . even whilst you sold arms to our Lord *himself*."

True, as well.

But this, at least, was worth a comment from the prisoner: "Your King, your *'Lord,'* is as vile a bag of filth as has ever dared rule his betters. He murders his own allies, and my only regret is that I did not charge him *double*."

The warden's eyes widened, furnace fire reflecting off the widened orbs. "You have tried to overthrow the Crown! You acted in outright conspiracy with His Majesty's enemies!"

McCullen's smile seemed to reflect neither fear nor outrage, rather amusement.

"Unlike your simpleton king," he said, "his enemies at least know that the destiny of the Clan McCullen is to *run* the wars, not simply to supply arms. Had your 'Lord' any brains at all, he would have come to me for more than rifles and powder."

Taken aback by his prisoner's unabashed bravado, the warden could only manage, almost sputtering, "Have you anything *else* to say before sentence is carried out?"

McCullen's smile disappeared. His eyes hardened, and his chin lifted.

"Yes, Warden, I do. I wish to state that the Clan

McCullen is far bigger, far more powerful, than any of you, or your pitiful rulers, could ever imagine."

"That's *enough* . . ."

The prisoner's eyes and nostrils flared, like a rearing horse. "My sons will continue to rise to power, long after I am gone. As will their sons, and, with God's grace, *their* sons." His unconcerned smile returned. "This shall not end with my death."

The warden had finally regained his poise, and the smile he bestowed his prisoner was laced with something sinister.

"Oh, your *death* is not why we are here, McCullen. We have no desire to make you a martyr. We're not going to *kill* you—we're going to make an *example* of you."

McCullen remained unimpressed.

Then the warden nodded to the prison workers, who removed the glowing metallic object from the fire, and finally the prisoner's face betrayed fear, terrible fear, as the metal mask was carried forth, toward him, its hinges opening with a ghastly creak. For the first time, McCullen struggled against the rack.

For what good it did him.

The warden, smiling now, in an ironically fatherly fashion said, "You will wear this mask, McCullen, until the day God calls for you. And until that day, no man, no woman, nor child shall ever see your treacherous face again. You will wear this mask for the term of your natural life . . . in my humble care."

The hot mask closed around his face as the bravery of the prisoner melted into screams, even as his flesh was seared, his face hidden from view . . .

. . . though the red square medallion at his throat maintained a stony, stoic silence, promising out of this heat a cold revenge against those who would condemn the leader of Clan McCullen to so undignified a fate.

"Whenever a new breed of evil emerges, a new breed of solider must fight it."

—GENERAL CLAYTON "HAWK" ABERNATHY

CHAPTER ONE
The Nobel War Prize

The skies were clear and bright outside NATO Headquarters in Brussels, the many colorful flags of the North Atlantic Treaty Organization's member nations flapping lazily in a gentle breeze, as if to say all was well with the world.

But within the massive, twentieth-century–modern central structure, in the auditorium-style seating of a darkened briefing chamber, twenty-two NATO military commanders and their aides were listening, some on translation headphones, to talk of war.

This talk, at least—courtesy of James McCullen of MARS Industries—posited warfare that might spare populaces of some of the carnage and destruction associated with history's favorite pastime.

This descendant, and namesake, of a certain James McCullen had a similarly strong, angular face and eyes that carried a similar proud defiance. His dark business suit was beautifully tailored to his slender, muscular frame, set off by the distinctive and unusual touch of a round red medallion of a tie tack that rode his silk tie.

No one present but McCullen himself had any reason to know that this was the symbol of an ancient Scottish clan that had made its fortune and fame in the sales of arms.

The man addressing these military commanders was in the same line of work, for which he made no apologies.

"Tragic as they are to fight," McCullen was saying, "wars *must* be won. Wars that linger and go on in a seemingly endless fashion destroy the social fabric of both sides of any conflict. If we can agree that wars are as inevitable as they are tragic, however, perhaps we can take steps to minimize their devastation. Perhaps these conflicts don't have to be as destructive as they have been in the past."

Behind the speaker at his sleek podium, on a huge wall screen, a series of complex schematics rolled continuously.

"*Nano-mites,*" McCullen said, biting off the words. "Perfect little soldiers. Originally developed, as you know, to isolate and destroy cancer cells . . . but we at MARS Industries . . . with the help of a little NATO funding . . ."

A few gentle laughs rippled. This audience knew how many billions had gone into "a little" funding; and the speaker seemed to soak up this benign, good-humored response.

". . . we discovered how to program them to do,

well, almost anything. What, for instance? How about . . . to *eat metal*."

On the looming screen behind McCullen, a soldier was remotely starting a tank before gunning it forward. Another soldier fired in response at the racing tank, using a shoulder-launched missile. The warhead struck the tank head on, bursting not into flame, rather into a shimmering silver wave that washed ripplingly over the metal, eating it away like a school of piranha devouring a horse.

With a gentle gesture, McCullen indicated this bizarre sight, saying, "What you see here are millions of microscopic nano-mites, ladies and gentlemen. Seven million, to be precise, the payload of a single warhead, with the ability to consume anything from a single tank, to an entire city."

The not-easily-impressed military minds gathered before McCullen were clearly startled, even shaken by what they were witnessing on the screen, which was the disappearance of a heavy tank with the silver nano-mites scurrying on toward a nearby jeep.

"No innocent casualties," McCullen said, with smooth salesmanship. "No loss of human life. Which is why the development of nano-mite technology has been such a priority for me and my company."

On screen, the soldier who fired the shoulder-launched warhead flicked a switch, and the nano-mites instantly went motionless around the jeep, as if they'd dropped dead.

"Once a target has been destroyed," McCullen said, "the launcher triggers a kill switch unique to each warhead, short-circuiting the nano-mites, preventing any *unwanted* destruction."

The entire chamber broke into applause.

Or rather, almost the entire chamber: retired Army General Clayton Abernathy—a handsome if hardened man in his early fifties, a grizzled veteran of countless battles, as the many ribbons on his dress uniform indicated—alone of the assemblage did not seem to be buying into McCullen's sales pitch.

From his seat at the back of the hall, with a lovely female aide just behind him, the dryly smiling man who was called General Hawk (by his friends and comrades and even his enemies) spoke up: "I guess this means you'll be the first arms dealer in history ever to be nominated for the Nobel Peace Prize."

That got some laughter going, but McCullen only smiled, his demeanor that of a good sport.

"Let's just say, General," McCullen said, with his own dry, if slightly sly smile, "I prefer the term 'armament solutions engineer.' "

This got some laughs, too.

One of the few *not* laughing was an individual known only as Zartan, McCullen's aide-de-camp—a tall, broad-shouldered man with black hair cut close to the scalp and an oval face whose handsome features bore a touch of cruelty. His dark business suit helped him blend into the sidelines, despite the distinctiveness of his appearance, which was a good thing, because Zartan had a habit that many might find disturbing.

McCullen's aide had a way of studying individuals and categorizing their tics and traits. As he recorded these in a computer-like mind, his face would reveal the process—one general in the audience would arch an eyebrow, and so would Zartan; another general would scratch an ear, and so would Zartan; another might laugh distinctively and so, quietly, would Zartan, the perfect natural mimic.

"Gentlemen," McCullen was saying, "I'm pleased to announce that tomorrow morning your first order of nanotech warheads will ship from my factory in Kyrgyzstan."

Again applause rang through the chamber.

Soon, followed by Zartan, the speaker exited the briefing room into a modern, beige-walled corridor where he paused briefly to shake hands with various supportive military commanders from around the world.

Not lost on James McCullen was the fact of General Hawk taking this all in.

At Hawk's side was his own aide-de-camp, Courtney Krieger, a lovely, statuesque young woman in the uniform of a Czech lieutenant, with the appearance of a fashion model belied by her somberly businesslike presence.

The general waited until McCullen had dealt with the well-wishers, then approached.

"Mr. McCullen," the general said. "Clayton Abernathy . . . if I might have a moment."

McCullen's smile seemed genuine enough as the two men shook hands.

"I know who you are, General Hawk. And from your questions and comments back there, I'd say you're as sharp in a briefing room as you are on the battlefield, if your reputation is to be believed."

"Not sure about that," Hawk said, offering the man his own good-natured smile. "You did provide an old soldier a broad target, and I guess I couldn't resist."

"Fair enough. At any rate, it's an honor to meet a military man of your many accomplishments."

With another smile and a nod, McCullen invited Hawk to walk along with him.

The two aides-de-camp fell in behind. Zartan stared unabashedly at the gorgeous Courtney Krieger, who walked alongside him. She noted, but did not comment on, these terrible manners.

McCullen was asking genially, "So what's on your mind, General?"

"Your warheads, sir." He shook his head with unhidden concern, even displeasure. "Securing them in transit is questionable to say the least . . . and how many ears in that room back there now know the when and the where of it?"

McCullen shrugged and smiled yet again, casually. "Those 'ears' all have top security clearance, General. You know that."

"And we both know what *that's* worth."

Trailing behind, the female aide-de-camp gave a sharp look to the male one.

"Are you mimicking me?" she demanded quietly.

Zartan flicked a half-smile. "Sorry. Bad habit."

Their bosses were talking, McCullen saying, "Look, General—delivery is my responsibility, and I assure you it's nothing I take lightly."

"I should hope not."

"I had NATO assign an elite American Special Forces unit to this task, a fully armored convoy with air support. I assure you, my warheads will be quite safe and secure."

Hawk walked along quietly, selecting his words carefully.

Then he said, with quiet force, "Sir, I have made a career of showing up where I'm needed . . . whether ordered to or not. And if your warheads are half as effective as your demonstration, and your words, indicate . . . then my team is definitely needed."

McCullen did not ask why an officially "retired" general would be offering a "team" in support in this situation.

"I appreciate the offer, General . . . but there is neither the time nor, frankly, the need for you and your people to play catch-up, here. The NATO team's been drilling for weeks—they're lit up and ready to roll."

Hawk touched the other man's arm and stopped him. Behind them, aides-de-camp stopped as well, not missing a beat.

"My unit," Hawk said with typically under-stated power, "does not need mission specific training. They have been chosen because of their ability to adapt to, and handle, any situation, no matter how unusual, no matter how extreme."

"I really appreciate this, General, your thoughtfulness, your willingness to get into this." McCullen smiled, but his eyes had a hardness. "Maybe next time. . . ."

McCullen began to move off, then stopped. "What did you say your unit was called again?"

"I didn't," Hawk said crisply. "I just said they were always ready."

McCullen's eyebrows rose, he smiled and nodded, then strode off. His aide-de-camp fell right in, but glanced back to throw a smile at the stunning young woman with whom he'd been walking.

"See you around," he said to her.

With a polite if icy smile, she said, "Not likely."

Zartan's smile remained but his eyes darkened; then he strode after his charge.

General Abernathy turned to his aide-de-camp, Courtney Krieger, whose code name was Cover Girl.

"Why don't I trust that man?" he asked her.

"Sir," she said, "I don't trust either of them."

CHAPTER TWO

Mother Goose Tail

Within the MARS Industries factory in Kyrgyzstan, Central Asia, four glassy warheads with glowing green payloads—each about the size of a softball—were being placed like particularly delicate eggs into the tray of a bulky, hardshell weapons case, each receiving a separate padded compartment.

Then the black-trimmed silver case—with its logo representing the Clan McCullen's red square medallion—was closed, and locked, and ready for transfer to the NATO delivery team.

In a locker room nearby, Captain Conrad R. Hauser—known to one and all as Duke—was strapping into body armor. He got into his full camouflage fatigues and attached an ammo clip onto his battle harness. With casual precision he loaded his HK416 Assault Rifle, and slung it over his shoulder.

He caught a glimpse of himself in a mirror, gave his image the briefest frown ("What are *you* looking at?"). He was tall, broad-shouldered, lithely muscular, and for a man in his early twenties had the appearance of a warrior who had already seen too much; perhaps it was the ragged scar under his right eye, though that did nothing to take away from his regular, even handsome features.

Delivery boy, he thought. *So many battles fought, so many comrades lost . . . and today I'm a delivery boy.*

Soon he and his fellow soldier (and best friend) Wallace "Ripcord" Weems were in the high-tech delivery bay of the MARS factory, dawn's early light finding its way through high windows of the vast yellow-trimmed, cement-floored chamber. Overseeing the impressively large, modern space were the red letters of MARS on a glowing white background.

The delivery bay's floor was striped red and occasionally yellow to demarcate areas, such as the one where the vehicles of this mission waited—two Cougar patrol vehicles and a massive armored Grizzly truck, all fitted with state-of-the-art rooftop weapons, one with a radar dish.

Right now, fifteen Special Forces soldiers in camouflage fatigues and body armor stood at attention in front of Duke, who still felt like a glorified delivery boy. He had not gotten into This Man's Army to bodyguard a damn briefcase, although this was apparently *some* damn briefcase, to justify this contingent of fighting men and firepower.

"All right," Duke said to the soldiers, "listen up. . . . The Cougars will be in front and back,

Grizzly in the middle, carrying the package. Minimum distances at all times—choppers will babysit. Understood?"

"Yes, sir," they said, their collective voices echoing in the cement chamber.

Their eyes were alert, their faces suitably hard and expressionless; these were good men, and Duke had no doubt that their cargo would be secure.

A four-man MARS security detail was escorting two lab workers in white contamination suits into the delivery bay; the lab workers' faces were bare in their hoods but their eyes were behind safety glasses.

The distinctive little group moved past the two trucks and armored vehicle, and one of the pair of lab coats stepped forward, though it was the other who bore the rugged-looking, hardshell case with the bold MARS logo.

"Captain Hauser?"

"Yes."

"We have the package."

"And I'm ready for delivery. Sergeant Weems?"

Ripcord—a lanky African American with a buzz-cut beard and shining eyes in his narrow, amiable face—stepped forward and took the case. Duke was signing off on the various forms.

Rip, whose confidence was matched by his charm and exceeded only by his courage, was more than just Duke's best friend—he was his "brother from another mother," and their tightness had its benefits . . . and its drawbacks.

One of the latter was a casualness with protocol from Rip that could irk Duke.

For example, right now Rip was grinning at the lead lab guy with an inappropriate jokiness, saying, "Not gonna blow up in my face, is it?"

The lab guy, anything but jokey, said, "That's impossible, Sergeant. They're not weaponized yet. And even so, there are kill switches inside."

"Kill switches, huh? Can't say I'm crazy about any switch with the word 'kill' attached."

"Understandable." Then the lab guy, deadpan, one-upped Rip: "I'd avoid potholes if I were you, Sergeant."

That shut Rip up, even as it widened his eyes, and Duke hid a smile as Rip passed the briefcase off to another soldier.

Rip noticed Duke's expression. "What are you lookin' at, Captain?"

"Nothing special."

Rip let that pass, and yelled, *"Mount up!"*

And the team mounted up, engines igniting, headlights snapping on, the morning sun still low in the east. The weapons case went into the armored Grizzly while Duke and Rip got into the lead Cougar, and the convoy rolled out into crisply cool daylight and the mountainous Central Asian terrain.

They were not alone. As the vehicles moved out of the heavily guarded factory gates, passing a sign

saying MILITARY ARMAMENTS RESEARCH SYNDI-
CATE, two Apache helicopters swooped in to pick
up their tail.

In back of their Cougar, two soldiers were remotely manning and panning a rooftop dual machine gun. Up front, behind the wheel, Ripcord
guided the vehicle along the winding mountain
road, while Duke was already checking in by radio.

"Mother Goose," Duke was saying, "this is Bird
Dog. We have the package, and are on the dot to
make Ganci Air Base at agreed-upon time."

He clicked off and waited, as Rip was smirking
over at him.

"You know," Rip said, griping good-naturedly
(which was his standard preset), "all this Mother
Goose, Bird Dog bull, I hate it, man. Why can't
they just let us say, 'Hey, Pete, it's Bill.' Assumin'
one of us is Pete and one of us is Bill."

"Not me," Duke said.

"Not you. You *like* this Mother Goose nonsense."

"Sure. Hell, I joined up for the jargon."

Rip gaped at him, and a voice on the radio said,
"Roger that, Bird Dog. Mother Goose out."

"I'm just sayin'," Rip said with a shrug, both
hands on the wheel. "Now, if I was in charge, if I
ran things? Why, I'd—"

Duke gave him a sideways glance. "Have strip-
per poles in the barracks? Tequila in our can-
teens?"

Rip grinned. "Whoever said you never have any

good ideas, Duke? If I wasn't drivin', I'd write those babies down!"

"I bet you would."

"And how about coed showers? There's another damn good idea. Don't let me forget *that* one."

"Oh, I won't." With a sigh that was part chuckle, Duke said, "Eyes on the road, Rip."

"Yessir, Captain."

They were winding through the Tian Shan mountain range with its fir forests contrasting beautifully with rocky gray. Sweeping through the skies, silhouetted by the rising sun, were the two Apache copters, the bodyguards for their well-armed delivery service.

On the rear Cougar, a radar dish kept up a vigilant sweep, and within a Special Forces soldier had his eyes locked on a radar monitor, which remained clear right now, but for the two steady signatures of those Apaches.

In the lead Cougar, Duke was on the radio again, saying, "Okay, Apaches—we are heavy. Keep those eyes open."

Throughout a long and tedious day, Duke and Rip did the same, as the narrow highway threaded through a mountain pass. Though their attention was on the road and their surroundings, this did not stop Rip from talking.

Nothing stopped Rip from talking.

As the cool blue shadows of dusk began to settle in, Rip said, "Hey, Duke! I been thinkin'."

"Haven't I warned you about that?"

"I got an idea."

"Which is why I warned you. Thinking can lead to ideas, and I have a lot of experience where your ideas can lead."

Rip ignored that. "I know where we should transfer next."

"You do, huh?"

"Weren't you bitchin' about being a glorified delivery boy on this thing?"

"I don't bitch. *You* bitch."

"Then you don't wanna know where I think we should transfer next?"

"Please don't say the Air Force."

"The Air Force!"

"I asked you not—"

"Perfect for us."

"I thought we were done with that discussion."

"Maybe *you* were done with it, Dukey boy. But not me. Look, I been flyin' since I was thirteen years old."

"Right, and sometimes you even had a plane. Anyway, buddy, I don't think your daddy's crop duster actually counts as flight hours logged."

"Jets, man, jets! Come on! You know I always qualify when I'm on leave."

"Tell you what," Duke said, his eyes still on alert, "you want to get up in the air? Hey, I'll buy you a damn trampoline."

"That is cold. That is brutal. Haven't we done ten years in the Army? Ain't it time to see if the grass is really greener in the Wild Blue Yonder?"

"Green in the blue? This continues to be the dumbest idea you've ever come up with, and that is saying something, that is *really* saying something. . . ."

"Funny, Duke. You're a real funny guy." Rip was pouting now, though he, too, remained alert. "Can't kill a brother's dreams, y'know."

Duke sighed. "Look, bro. I just don't wanna transfer to the Air Force, okay? That's your dream. Not mine."

"Give me one good reason."

With no kidding in his tone, Duke said earnestly, "I want to be on the ground . . . *in* the thick of it. In the fight. Not flying *over* it."

"Plane can land, and *get* in it."

"Plane can also crash. I like something under my feet besides a couple inches of sheet metal and air."

Rip said nothing for five seconds—a new record. "Well, I gotta level with ya, man—my application? It's all filled out."

"All filled out, huh? And they accept applications made out that way?"

"What way?"

"In crayon?"

Rip shook his head. "Cold. You are one cold dude, Duke." He gazed longingly into the sky. "When I die, I wanna come back as a bird . . . where I can soar and sail free . . . and come back and crap white stuff all over your damn car."

Duke smiled a little.

He would not have been smiling had he seen the ominous dark shape that suddenly dropped in behind both the Apaches and the convoy itself. Even had he seen this shape, Duke couldn't have known what he was looking at, blurred by engine exhaust as it was.

But in pursuit.

In pursuit.

Yet within the rear Cougar, the soldier whose eyes were on the radar screen saw only the two signatures of those Apache copters, maintaining their position.

Nothing else.

When Rip hit a pothole, right after the Grizzly bearing the briefcase had done the same thing, the kidding-on-the-square words of that lab guy jumped back into both their minds.

Then Rip glanced at a farming community at the base of hillside, his eyes lingering a few seconds.

"Hey, Duke—them cows?"

"What about the cows?" This was a new line of discussion, even for Rip.

"They look lonely."

"The cows look lonely."

Rip's eyes, narrowed, turned toward Duke. "On the training run . . . wasn't there a bunch of damn villagers around here?"

Duke snapped to attention . . .

. . . but too late.

That dark, unseen presence trailing both them and their Apache chaperones was moving even closer. Two concussion cannons slid out of ports on either side of the black shape, and began firing, simultaneously—not conventional shells, rather subatomic blasts. . . .

The first of these punched into the nearest Apache and crumpled the whirlybird the way a frat boy crushes a beer can on his forehead. Only then did the chopper explode, like a big fat firecracker, falling in a swirl of smoke, flame, and shrapnel.

In the lead Cougar, both Duke and Rip could see the flaming ball of metal as it crashed onto the armored vehicle ahead of them, instantly blocking the convoy's path. Just as fast, Rip hit the brakes.

"Jesus Christ!" Rip blurted. "Bird down!"

"Back up, buddy," Duke said, urgent but cool. "Back up!"

Rip did, while into the radio, Duke bit off words: "Mother Goose, this is Bird Dog. We are under attack. Repeat, we are *under attack*! One Apache down. Roadway blocked!"

Dusk was turning into night as the second Apache pivoted to finally notice that dark shape, which as it revealed itself was like nothing any of the convoy soldiers had ever seen. . . .

At first glance, it seemed to be a massive helicopter; but there were no rotors—instead, the thing hovered, thanks to half a dozen jet thrusters. In days to come, the craft would be known as a Typhoon Gunship. For now, it was merely a nightmare.

But the soldiers of the convoy, battle-seasoned as they were, were used to waking nightmares, and the remaining Apache hosed the Typhoon with its six-barreled mini-guns.

The rounds, however, bounced off the Typhoon's angled armor like bullets off Superman's chest.

And when the strange craft's concussion cannons let loose on the second Apache, the blasts caught the copter head on, and crumpled it like a wadded ball of paper that became a flaming orb that went reeling ass-over-tail-rotor into the roadway near the rear Cougar, hemming in the convoy.

The Grizzly up front launched two heat-seeking missiles off its roof-turret back at the Typhoon, which almost offhandedly fly-swatted them down. The big black craft let loose with more subatomic blasts, taking out the rear Cougar, flattening it like a paper cup under a heel, and doing the same to every tree within a hundred feet on either side of the roadway.

All of this Duke could see in his rearview mirror, even as Rip guided the Cougar in reverse.

They could see the concussion blast—which had brushed past them—flipping the Grizzly like a thumb flicking a coin; the big armored vehicle landed hard, its windows shattering from the assault, creating thousands of lethal glass shards shooting within the vehicle, killing the drivers with countless cutting wounds.

Then the Typhoon fired again, and Rip tried to maneuver the Cougar but the blast sideswiped them, and sent the vehicle—and them—tumbling end over end.

And as he was going around and around, all Duke could think was, *"Delivery boy, my backside. . . ."*

CHAPTER THREE

Watched Like a Hawk

When the Cougar stopped rolling, Duke and Ripcord found themselves on the upturned ceiling, feeling like a pair of dice some gambler gave a damn good shake before going for broke.

Duke's first thought was the two guys in back of the vehicle, who'd been remotely manning and panning the rooftop dual machine gun that had been reduced to scrap metal in the crash. But both men had apparently been killed instantly when the subatomic blast caved in the Cougar's armor.

"Rip!" Duke said. "You okay, man?"

"Yeah—unless that's blood I feel drippin' on the back of my skull. . . ."

It was.

Duke checked out the injury. "It's messy but you'll live. We gotta get out of this baby before it blows."

"What the hell hit us?"

As if by way of answer, a roar announced the black Typhoon as it hovered near their crashed vehicle, stirring up roadside dust. Suddenly Duke knew how an animal caught in a trap felt.

Rip blurted, "What the hell is *that*?"

"*Who* the hell is that? . . . Come on. . . ."

Duke grabbed onto Ripcord and began dragging him out into the waiting night, away from the party crashers.

A side door on the hovering craft hissed open, revealing half a dozen foot soldiers clad in black battle armor, menacing figures and a variety of fighter known to their masters as Vipers. Their battle helmets covered their heads with a shape and shielding that gave them a bizarrely skull-like aspect, down to the deep dark holes where their eyes should be.

The fearsome, formidable Vipers were all armed the same way—with futuristic, nasty-looking rifles whose snouts promised very big paydays.

Charging down metal steps from the Typhoon, the Vipers began to fan out in the moon-washed landscape, clearly intending to kill any survivors of the destruction they'd wrought. Affixed to their rifle barrels were bright lights that could cut through the night.

The several surviving Special Forces guys in the remains of the crashed Grizzly began to unload on the intruders with their assault rifles, muzzle flashes like fireflies in the darkness. But their armor-penetrating slugs had zero impact on the next-gen body armor of the Vipers.

And when the Vipers fired back, those high-tech

rifles threw not bullets but a powerful pulsing charge that crushed the Special Forces soldiers, armor and all, flinging their dead bodies like discarded refuse along the roadway.

From the Typhoon emerged another figure—not a foot soldier, no mere Viper, but a woman known in certain circles as the Baroness, and in others, simply as Ana.

Two qualities in her were so evident that no one could miss them, even on first glance.

First, she was very beautiful, exotically so, with long, straight brunette hair brushing the shoulders of her black formfitting body armor, though her big brown eyes were largely hidden behind sleek night-vision-tinted safety glasses. The neckline of the body armor exposed the upper part of her swelling bosom, an exposure of flesh that arrogantly dared bullets to try for her, as if she could walk blithely invulnerable across the battlescape.

Second, she was very dangerous, her expression as cold as that of any battle-hardened veteran, two lethal-looking oversized pistols at her hips, gunslinger style, emphasized by the low-slung belt that bore a buckle big enough for a pirate, and the same could be said for her high black boots.

The woman called Ana strode menacingly toward the crashed Grizzly, her eyes unblinking behind the protective glasses, which glinted off the fires of the crashed copters on the periphery. She took in the dark world around her—the scrubby roadside rising to a nearby forest worthy of Snow

White, with its skeletal branches like the knobby fingers of witches, and its spooky ground fog mingling with the darker smoke of crashed, burning vehicles.

The two Special Forces soldiers who'd been responsible for launching heat-seeking missiles at the Typhoon had survived the Grizzly's crash. In its crumpled remains, they did their best to maintain cover. But when the female warrior walked toward them, with what seemed to them the clear intention of taking the prize that was the weapons briefcase they were guarding, the two soldiers jack-in-the-boxed up and took aim with their rifles.

With a two-handed quick draw that would have staggered Wyatt Earp, the woman in black summoned her pistols, and they too shot not bullets but a pulsing force that crushed both soldiers, *Boom!*, *Boom!*, armor, weapons, flesh and blood.

Ana flipped her big pulse pistols back into her holsters even as a Viper blew the back door off the fallen Grizzly with his pulse rifle. She climbed into the upside-down wreckage, which resembled a modern art sculpture more than a vehicle, but the well-padded briefcase was unharmed. She moved blithely, even gracefully, around the corpses of Special Forces soldiers and plucked the weapons case from its resting place.

Not far from there, Duke was carrying Rip over his shoulders, like a sack of grain he was hauling, running like hell, or anyway trying to.

Rip muttered, "Duke?"

"Shut up. I'm busy."

"Just wanna say . . . if I die?"

"You're not gonna die."

"I just want you to know . . . if I die? It's 'cause you never *could* run worth a damn."

"Jesus, Rip!" His friend was heavy, and his legs were hurting, as he ran across rocky ground, looking for cover. "Give a guy a break!"

"I'm just sayin'," Rip said, as they bumped along, "be nice if you could move a tad faster. Bad guys look like they can *move.* . . ."

"Bad guys . . . aren't . . . carrying a couple hundred pounds . . . of fertilizer!"

"Cold. You are cold."

Duke made no response to that, because that was when the crashed Cougar they'd recently vacated chose to blow itself to smithereens, in a concussive blast that sent Duke tumbling, and Rip with him, in an ass-over-tea-kettle roll that dumped them into a ditch.

This caught the attention of Ana, who touched the stem of her glasses, which had the ability to zoom in, revealing a close view of Duke, peering up over the lip of the ditch. This made her smile, though there was nothing humorous or friendly in it.

Down in the ditch, Duke rolled over and gave Rip a quick look. His friend appeared dazed and generally pretty well messed up. But at least that wound on the back of Rip's head wasn't streaming blood.

"Stay here," Duke said.

"What am I, your damn dog? . . . Where the hell you *goin'*?"

"When they hire me to deliver something, I damn well deliver it."

"Huh?"

"Buddy, I'm gettin' that package."

Duke leapt to his feet and hauled butt down the ditch.

Rip, alone now, felt cold and sick and, though he would never admit it to a living soul, afraid. Then he sensed someone, or something, nearby, and he whirled and looked into a grotesque face, a monster's face, and he screamed like a Girl Scout whose cookies had been snatched from her.

The "monster"—a cow that had found its way down into the ditch in all the confusion—just stared at Rip.

Recovering from the shock, realizing that the cow was just a cow, Rip muttered to himself, "Least I ain't *alone*. . . ."

In a crouch, Duke had run a distance in the ditch and now was sprinting up the embankment. He almost ran directly into one of the enemy soldiers, face-to-face now with a Viper, who raised his pulse rifle and was about to blow Duke to Kingdom Come. . . .

But a slender, black-gloved hand clamped down on the pulse rifle's barrel, and lowered it, in the manner of a schoolteacher correcting a child.

The skeleton-head Viper whipped a glance at the woman in black beside him, and any objection he'd been about to make went away, as if a switch had been thrown.

Duke was looking at this lethal beauty himself. He had a good game face, in most instances, but now that had dissolved into shocked recognition . . . and not just because she carried in one dark-gloved hand the cargo entrusted to him, the warheads weapons case. . . .

Touching the temple of her glasses and turning off the night-vision tint revealed the full beauty of those big brown eyes. This in itself shook Duck: Those eyes had once been blue, as the hair had been blonde. But it was her . . . it *was* her. . . .

Her hardened expression seemed to shift into something softer, if hesitantly so.

"Hello, Duke," she said, her voice throaty, and as lovely as she was.

Then that soft look vanished as, without even taking her hand off the Viper's gun barrel, she roundhouse kicked Duke, her boot kissing his face . . . and knocking him on his tail.

She looked down at him. "Have to admit—you had that coming."

Duke gazed up at a woman he had once known very well. And he could read her expression, as she struggled with something; then any hint of mercy disappeared as a hard expression again took hold.

She removed her hand from the Viper's rifle, flicked him a look of permission, as the brown eyes went to the man she'd once known; and there was apology, even regret, in them as she said, "Good-bye, Duke. . . ."

Normally Duke would have jumped either the woman or the soldier, but something inside him was curling up and wanting to die.

How could she do this *to him?*

But the Viper did not fire, because his attention—and that of his battle mistress—was on something behind Duke, something they all heard before they saw it, Duke turning away from his own pending execution to see what the fuss was about. . . .

It was about this: A transport was rocketing down onto the scene, a distinctive craft that wore a green-camo skin on a body that was sharklike right down to its snout, with four-winged jet thrusters riding high. The craft—known to those who used it as a Howler—rotated ninety degrees, slowing into a hover.

Whether this was good guy reinforcements or more bad guys, Duke had no way to know—he certainly didn't recognize the craft and could discern no markings of any government.

There was nothing left but for Duke to get back in the game, which he did, taking the opportunity to leap to his feet and smash a forearm into the Viper's throat and send him and his high-tech rifle onto the dirt.

The woman in black wanted none of this—not Duke, certainly not the hovering Howler—and she turned and raced off like the thoroughbred she was . . . taking the weapons case with her.

A figure in black came quickly down a rope from the transport, landing nimbly just behind a Viper, whose neck he snapped with lethal ease, a chef halving a stalk of celery.

Damn, this guy is quick, Duke thought, his eyes barely able to follow the blur of the black-clad figure as the ninja-like figure drew a samurai sword, a katana, from a shoulder sheath, and buried its blade in another adversary with ceremonial skill.

Duke could see another Viper, too far away for the ninja's blade to reach, who was aiming one of those pulse rifles at this new arrival. But before Duke could even call out a warning, the man he would come to know as Snake Eyes did a gun-fighter quick draw and fired a Glock right at the Viper.

Duke might have warned him that these guys had body armor that couldn't be pierced . . . only Snake Eyes had already taken that into account, and his bullet found access through the eye slit of the Viper's skull-like helmet. And, as Duke well knew, a head shot was the best shot in any case. . . .

All of this had happened very quickly—Snake Eyes had been on the scene for maybe six seconds.

Duke watched this almost otherworldly figure as Snake Eyes sheathed his sword and holstered his smoking Glock. On the triceps of the man's black body armor were red ninja clan markings, his face hidden by a black armor mask (which did not include the fatal eye-slit flaw of his opponents). In a night now filled with the tracer streaks of gunfire, Snake Eyes took off after more prey.

That boy, Duke thought, *is one righteous bad dude. . . .*

Then he took off himself, but in the direction Ana had gone, into the nearby fir forest. Soon his eyes, at least, had caught up with her, and he could make out the weapons case in her grasp. All around her, and him, pulse bursts and tracer fire were ripping up trees.

Rip's Air Force had arrived.

Duke was unaware that a Viper was lining him up in gun sights. But an arrow with laser-like speed and accuracy ripped through the Viper's eye slit and added insult to injury, by both taking out an eye and delivering an electric charge that fried him better than an electric chair.

The unknowing Duke had been saved by another lethal young woman—Shana O'Hara, whose code name in a certain secret international peacekeeping organization was "Scarlett"—positioned in the hatchway of the Howler.

Now the red-haired beauty, also in black body armor, came quickly down a rope with her gaspropulsion crossbow pistol in hand, ready to take out more Vipers.

Quickly she learned that her exploding arrows could not penetrate the enemy combatant's body armor, but they did knock the bastards down, not killing them, just taking them out of the action, for a while at least.

One Viper recovered soon enough to raised his weapon her way, and Scarlett ducked behind the crashed Grizzly.

Her crossbow pistol's viewfinder snapped an image of the Viper's face armor, and she quickly targeted his eye slit on her pistol's LED screen. Then she fired not at the Viper, but in the opposite direction, the arrow bolt flying away as if on a trip of its own volition.

The Viper did not blast in the opposite direction, no, he sent a powerful pulse impact right her way, crushing the vehicle's mangled body further, and knocking Scarlett to the ground, hard, her crossbow pistol thrown from her grip. The weapon, on the earth ten feet or so away, taunted her.

She crawled for it.

But the Viper cut her off, and aimed down at her, right at her head. He was about to fire when he heard an odd whisper behind him, glanced its way, and the smart arrow Scarlett had launched found his eye slit and took him out, exploding itself into nothing and the Viper into vapor.

Another Viper, seeing this, bolted toward home, the Typhoon that had brought him.

But the hovering Howler had a nasty surprise for him: a big, burly African American in black body armor and wielding a huge weapon, a combo machine gun/grenade launcher, leaned out and displayed a grin that was almost as frightening to behold as the weapon.

"Time to lay down some bottom end!" Hershel Dalton shouted with grim enthusiasm.

The big man had handsome, angular features and his hair was cut close to his skull. His code name in the secret organization was Heavy Duty, and his shoulder ammo belt bore an HD by way of identification.

Heavy Duty fired a grenade, *boom!,* and caught the Viper broadside, flinging him out of view, almost as if he'd never been there.

Now the two vehicles engaged, the Typhoon firing at Heavy Duty in its hatchway, and the Howler nimbly firing its left-side thrusters, rolling itself onto its side. The Typhoon's concussive blasts whipped past, decimating a patch of forest.

Heavy Duty, however, had been taken for an interesting ride, and now was hanging awkwardly out of the hatchway; nonetheless, he managed to fire off a double blast of grenades . . .

. . . which the Typhoon's mini-gun quickly shot out of the air, skeet shoot style.

As impressive as the enemy craft's display was, the Howler topped it, following with missiles that struck the Typhoon's concussion cannons, ripping them apart, and shaking the ship like a naughty child.

Still back in the ditch with his bovine companion, Ripcord—feeling better, his head clear—was firing his assault rifle at Vipers while massive tracer fire flashed past them both.

"Watch the cow!" Rip advised his adversaries

crossly. "Watch the damn cow! You want it to rain *hamburger*?"

Elsewhere, the Baroness was racing toward the Typhoon, which was trying to recover from the Howler's assault. Duke was closing in on her, despite a hail of pulse fire from Vipers; his pistol was in hand.

"Ana!" he called.

He charged at her like a bull, tackled her, and then she was sprawling on the ground, the briefcase of warheads tumbling free, before it skidded to a stop. For a long moment, the man and the woman were eye to eye, each demanding an explanation from the other without quite knowing the question.

Then Duke scrambled after the case, while Heavy Duty was laying down cover, spraying gunfire toward the woman in black, keeping her back.

Heavy Duty advised her: "I hate killing women, lady! Back the hell off! Don't make me *do* it. . . ."

But a grappling line slammed into the ground, right in front of Ana, and she leapt for it, grabbed hold, and it pulled her up and through the trees, and up through a round access port in the deck of the Typhoon.

Then the strange craft was disappearing over a rise.

She had escaped, and she and her people (if those soldiers *were* people) had done plenty of damage . . . but Duke had wound up with the case.

The cacophony of battle stilled. Silence draped

the roadside battlefield with the ominous, somber tone of death. The three warriors in black body armor who had come to Duke's aid approached him. Slowly but confidently.

But he couldn't be sure about them—Ana had been in similar body armor, hadn't she?—and he whirled to take all of them in, pistol in hand, eyes and nostrils flaring.

"Stand down!" he demanded. "Stand the hell down!"

The massive African American moved slowly forward, his big, bulky yet sleekly designed weapon still in his hands. "Lower your weapon, sir. We're not hostiles. We're not the enemy."

"Pointing guns at me," Duke said, "doesn't make much of a case for that."

A smaller man, trimly bearded—his black body armor a computerized surveillance suit, with more gizmos than a Swiss Army Knife, including an eyepiece computer screen and mic that tied him into the ship—hopped out of the Howler. This was Abel Shaz, code name: Breaker, and he held out a hand to Duke.

And not for a handshake.

Breaker's accent, French North African, was something Duke recognized, though the smaller man's words might as well have been in a foreign language: "Sir! Please hand over that case."

"I don't know who you are, buddy," he told the newcomer. Then he went from face to face saying,

"I don't know who *any* of you are. And I sure don't know who *they* are . . ."

He indicated to the fallen Vipers around them.

". . . but I do know that until I find out, I'm not lowering my weapon or handing over anything to you, or anybody not connected directly to the U.S. military."

The big black guy, frowning as if vaguely offended, said, "If it weren't for us, pal, you'd be greased along with the rest of your boys. Now hand that damn thing *over*!"

The answer came not from Duke, but from somewhere in the shadows: *click-clack*.

Both Duke and his supposed rescuers all knew the sound of a weapon cocking for action.

Rip stepped up into view with his rifle poised to fire. No nonsense, he said, "What's your unit?"

The redheaded woman said, "That's classified."

"Yeah? Well, I classify that response as bullshit."

Duke caught sight of the masked ninja discreetly fingering shuriken throwing stars on his belt; but Duke also saw the redhead give the man a look that made his hand move away from the deadly little weapons.

The smaller one, with the headset, said, "Someone would like a word with you."

He set a small round object on the ground near Duke, who had no idea that the thing was a holo-projector, at least not until one second later, when it produced a three-dimensional image of a sternly handsome fighting man in his fifties, whom Duke did not recognize.

This was General Hawk in beret, black body armor jacket and camo-fatigues, so real he might have been standing there before them, with only the lack of shadows he cast in the moonlight to betray him as a hologram.

"State your name and rank, soldier," the commanding figure said.

This was no military uniform that Duke had ever seen, and he saw no reason not to say, "After you." He did not even attach "sir" to it.

"My team just saved your behind, son. This is where *you* say, 'Thank you.' "

" 'Thank you' aren't the two words that come to mind just now," Duke said. "I wasn't told about any support for this mission, so you better tell your team to stand down."

Next to Duke, Rip and his rifle stood at the ready, a one-man firing squad.

"Hey," Rip said, "after what I been through? Happy to turn this fine night into a turkey shoot."

The hologram image of the general was handed a file, from off-projector. He glanced down at it.

"Easy, Ripcord," the hologram said.

Rip's eyebrows went up, but his guard did not go down. "How do *you* know *me*?"

"*How* I know isn't important. *What* I know is— expert marksman, second best in your battalion, weapons specialist, jet-qualified . . ."

Flicking a sideways glance at Duke, Rip said, "I *told* you—"

"As for who I am," the hologram said, "I'm General Clayton Abernathy. You may have heard of me . . . Duke."

That he knew Duke was no surprise, after Rip's background had been reeled off.

"You're General Hawk," Duke said with a crisp nod. "Afghanistan, NATO Forward Command . . ."

Breaker seized this moment of detente to step close enough, if gingerly, to sweep a scanner across the hardshell weapons case.

Hawk's hologram smiled at Duke, a twinkle in its eyes. "NATO was my *last* job, soldier. I'm with a whole new outfit now."

Duke swiveled his gun toward Breaker—specifically toward his head.

Breaker flinched and said, "Just need to deactivate its tracking beacon, as a security measure."

Hawk said, "Hand over that weapons case, son, and let us deliver those warheads. You can see the superiority of our arms and numbers. We can get those warheads where they're supposed to go."

"All due respect, sir," Duke said, "no way. I signed for 'em, I carried 'em, I'll deliver 'em. My mission, my package."

Breaker's scanner beeped, and he keyed a button, halting the beeping.

Then he threw a little look at Duke and said, as if to a child, "Now, that wasn't so hard, was it?"

The Hawk hologram said, "I understand your

desire to complete your mission, Captain, and deliver that package. And it's fine as far as it goes. But you seem to be a little short on transportation at the moment. Team Alpha will deliver you to me, and we will work that out."

Duke hiked an eyebrow. "And where exactly *are* you, sir?"

"Come see for yourself," the hologram said with a smile, and flickered out.

Rip glanced at Duke. "We *could* use wheels. That general's for real?"

"The *real* him is," Duke said. He made a decision. "A great man, a great hero. I trust him."

Rip shrugged. "Then I trust him." Then he whispered: "Dibs on the redhead."

Duke rolled his eyes, then followed Alpha Team to the hovering Howler. But he allowed no one else to carry that briefcase. At the moment, he might only be a delivery boy for Uncle Sam; but when he carried a package, he delivered a package.

CHAPTER FOUR

Government Issue

As the Howler moved through the night, Duke and Rip were strapped in, seated with their hosts in a semicircular fashion at the rear of the craft.

Duke had the weapons case on his lap, but Rip was getting some TLC from the redhead whom the others were calling Scarlett. She leaned in, hovering over Rip, tending to the wound on the back his head, cleaning it gently.

Openly flirtatious, Rip kidded her: "Y'know, you just may be the cutest stewardess I ever saw."

An eyebrow went up over one of the light-blue eyes. "The last guy who talked to me like that—"

From his seat, Heavy Duty advised Rip, "You don't wanna call Scarlett 'cute.' "

Breaker, also strapped in and seated, said, "Yeah, man, I would *definitely* not call her 'cute.' "

Then the ninja was at Rip's side, shoving a drip needle into his arm, with the bedside manner of an assassin. Rip gave him the hairy eyeball while stifling a yelp.

The redhead was amused. "I thought all you Special Ops types were tough."

"We *are* tough . . . but we also *sensitive*."

Snake Eyes rested a hand on Scarlett's shoulder and gave her a slow nod, which she returned.

"Yeah," she told the ninja. "I got this."

The ninja gave her shoulder a squeeze and returned to his seat. The intimacy of the moment between Scarlett and Snake Eyes was not lost on Rip. She caught him staring at both of them, and he quickly moved his gaze to the big black guy they called Heavy Duty.

"Hey, bro," Rip said, taking in the clipped-to-skull hair on the big man's skull, "that's some real-life lookin' peach fuzz you got goin' on there. . . ."

He reached to teasingly touch it and Heavy Duty stretched out a hand and caught Rip's and squeezed it.

Hard.

". . . not to mention, some kung-fu grip, my brother."

Rip, once he'd had his hand handed back, settled in his seat and glanced at Duke, beside him.

Duke said to one and all, "What kind of outfit *is* this? Not regular Army, based on the accents." He met Scarlett's eyes. "You're a Canadian . . ." He met Heavy Duty's eyes now. "And you're British . . ." Now he caught Breaker's gaze. "And I make French North Africa. Algiers?"

"Morocco," Breaker said. "Where were *you* born?"

Rip snorted a laugh. "You kiddin' me? Duke here wasn't born—he was Government Issued!"

Nobody laughed; nobody even smiled.

Duke turned to the hooded ninja. "And what about you? Where do you hail from? Since you don't say much, I can't nail an accent."

Scarlett said, "He doesn't talk."

Rip asked, "Why not?"

But it was Breaker who answered: "He never said."

Duke was studying them, his eyes traveling from face to face. "Yet somehow you're all in the same unit. One you can't share the *name* of with me . . . right?"

Scarlett said, "Not without getting tossed out for telling."

Rip grinned and said mockingly, "Duke, buddy, don't you get it? Why, these are super-secret *Mission: Impossible* types. This whole thing is all gonna self-destruct in, like, five—"

"You're gonna go after them," Duke said, cutting off Rip and speaking to the team around them.

Nobody spoke.

But Duke knew. "You *are,* aren't you? You're going after the ones who hit my convoy. You're gonna get the bastards, right?"

Again silence, though Heavy Duty and Scarlett traded the quickest knowing looks.

"Then," Duke said, "whoever the hell you are, whatever the hell this damn unit is . . . *I want in.*"

Heavy Duty shook his head. "Not our call."

Rip tried to sit up straight; the stuff going into his arm seemed to be making him woozy. He gave Scarlett a goofy look. "I want in, too. That way you and me can spend some quality time together. . . ."

A sword whipped the air perhaps an inch from Rip's startled face. Rip swallowed, glanced toward the ninja, who appeared to be innocently checking out his blade.

But Rip got the message . . . he did get the message. . . .

Scarlett's eyes went to Duke's, then flicked to Rip and back again. "Are you two some kind of team?"

"Some kind," Duke admitted.

Rip put in, "We been together forever . . . put your eyes back in your head, honey. It's not *that* way. I am strictly interested in the gender that you do such a nice job of representing. By the way, hi . . . my name's Ripcord."

She smirked at him. "*Nobody's* name is Ripcord."

"Well, it's what they call me."

"Why do they call you that?"

Breaker, who at that moment happened to be checking Rip's files on his ball-like eyepiece computer monitor, laughed and said, "They call him that because his *name* is Wallace Weems!"

And a miracle happened: Somebody had shut Rip up.

Everyone caught some z's and by the time they started waking up, sunlight was streaming in, and the Howler was skimming over the Great Pyramids

of Giza, catching the attention of a camel caravan
heading into the golden desert at a considerably
lesser speed than the transport that was blur-
ring by.

Also observing the Howler, in a security room
below the sandy surface, were eight security technicians in camo-fatigues seated around an island
console in a small, windowless room. As they
worked their keyboards, they watched a holographic image of the Howler as it soared across the
dunes.

A tech hit a large switch on his console and said,
"Alpha-One, this is Base. You are cleared for
entry."

A mammoth sand dune directly in front of the
approaching Howler spiraled like a whirlpool, finally opening to reveal a cavernous port. The
Howler's thrusters twisted vertically and the craft
dropped like a helicopter into the hole in the
desert, descending until it could set down on a
landing platform swathed in darkness. Only after
the roof had spiraled shut again did the flood lights
switch on.

The Howler's hatchway opened and the team
stepped down and out, followed by a hesitant Rip
and Duke, the latter still carrying the hardshell
weapons case.

From the shadows came the voice of General
Hawk: "Welcome to the Pit, gentlemen!"

From behind the lights, General Hawk and his
lovely blonde aide-de-camp strode out to greet

them. Hawk wore a brown leather jacket with a green T-shirt, camouflage trousers, and the trademark angled beret bearing the profile of a falcon and a single star, in black against gold—an insignia Duke had never seen in any military branch.

Even the female aide wore camo-fatigues, which appeared to be standard attire at the Pit, though nothing could camouflage her slender, willowy beauty.

Hawk handed a dossier he'd been reading to his aide, who carried a tablet-sized computer in one hand, and stepped forward to shake hands with Duke, whom he addressed by name.

"Sir," Duke responded.

"I've read a lot about you two," the general said, glancing at Ripcord.

Rip, defensively, said, "Okay, now, look, 'steal' is a harsh word. I didn't exactly 'steal' that Blackhawk, it was more like I *borrowed* it. . . ."

Ignoring this and primarily giving his attention to Duke, the general said, "Matter of fact, according to our files, one of my subordinates tried to recruit you to our little operation, Captain, awhile back."

Duke frowned. "I was never asked to join any Op group."

"Perhaps you'll recall a tall gentleman approaching you in Thailand, when you were on leave . . . what was it, four years ago?"

Duke's eyebrows flicked upward. "Yeah. I do."

"Right before you tore up that bar?"

Rip said, "Four years back, my boy here had issues. Fact, even his *issues* had issues. And you will need to be specific about *which* tore-up bar you are talkin' about."

Duke didn't like the road they were going down, and shifted gears: "General, this doesn't look like any Tac Op I've ever seen. Where are we exactly?"

Hawk thought about that momentarily. Then he said, "All right . . . you trusted me. I'll trust you."

A loud metallic clang put a startling period on the end of the general's sentence, as the platform began to descend. Duke and Rip watched, impressed, as they passed an Urban Combat Level, where men and women were training with next-gen urban warfare equipment in a cement cityscape.

"Technically," Hawk said, "G.I. JOE doesn't exist. But if it did, it would be comprised of the top men and women from the best military units all over the world. The alpha dogs . . ."

Their host was interrupted by the striking sight of an attractive young woman zipping into a jumpsuit that made her damn near invisible.

"Camouflage suit," the general explained. "Reflects and refracts light. Essentially, you blend into the background."

"Oh man," Rip said. "I want me one of those babies."

Breaker said, "What, the suit or the girl?"

Rip blinked. "What suit?"

Scarlett rolled her eyes, and Rip grinned at her, saying, "Jealous already?"

The general seemed oblivious to all this, and was continuing: "Ten nations signed on in the first year. Working together, sharing intel. Now . . . we are up to twenty-three."

Duke was taking in the urban combat training. These same sleek black jumpsuits, common to the Howler team, seemed to be standard G.I. JOE issue. Since Duke and Rip were dressed similarly, they already seemed to fit right in.

Of course, the body armor *these* folks had was something else again.

Duke said, "I've never seen combat gear like yours. What's the trick?"

Scarlett said, "Liquid armor."

Duke and Rip exchanged glances. *Yeah*, that *explains it. . . .*

The next level they passed had a Sea World look, as dozens of men and women were testing fantastic underwater vehicles in huge tanks, supervisors watching and annotating on tablet-sized handheld computers, like Hawk's aide carried.

"Deep Sea Combat Level," the general explained.

Duke asked, "You called this place . . . or your organization or whatever it is . . . G.I. JOE. That's an old American term. Goes back to World War Two. But this is an international setup, right?"

"Right. And it goes far beyond the individual na-

tional interests of its members. We are targeting
not rogue states so much as a new generation of
super-criminal organizations that feed and fund
rogue states."

"And you've kept it all off the international
media's radar?"

"We've been pretty successful so far, yes. That's
the good news—the bad news is, whenever we
manage to shut down one organization, another
springs up in its place."

Soon they were off the platform and being led by
General Hawk into the Control Room of the Pit,
the area that had no doubt inspired the "Pit" des-
ignation, a cavernous circular chamber half of
which was ringed with workstations where countless smaller monitors echoed larger nearby wall-
mounted flat-screens. The gray marble floor and
blue-tinged sloping ceiling fought for dominance
with the green-hued wall monitors, and a dome
light illuminated a central, circular workstation
where the general could display maps or charts or
simply set down a cup of coffee.

The rest of the chamber was arrayed with
slightly smaller wall monitors and an elevated ob-
servation post, hemmed by a crosshatching of
metal railing. The real work was going on opposite
this post, technicians at their stations while the
many monitors, large and small, constantly shifted
images and information.

One of these techs said to the general, "Mr. Mc-
Cullen's standing by, sir."

"Patch him through, please," Hawk said.

Duke turned to the general's beautiful aide. "So . . . do we know who hit us out there?"

"Currently unidentified," she said.

Heavy Duty, behind them, said, "And how the hell did they get a jump jet like ours?"

"Whoever they are," Scarlett said, "they have some highly classified intel, and state-of-the-art weaponry, too. Which means, they have a hell of a lot of money behind them."

Cover Girl nodded crisply. "Their capabilities are beyond anything we've encountered."

"And that," Rip put in, "is the one and only reason we got our asses handed to us."

Duke said nothing about having recognized the female leader of the enemy group. General Hawk's eyes were on him, and Duke could only wonder if Hawk already knew. . . .

"We need to find out everything we can about that female commander of theirs," the general said, as if reading Duke's mind. "*Knowing* is always half the battle."

Rip blinked. "What's the other half?"

Before anyone could answer Rip, a figure materialized like a ghost beside him—a slender man with an angular-featured face in a dark tailored suit with a distinctive red medallion tie tack at his neck—*and walked right through Ripcord!*

Rip blurted an expletive, but then he—like everyone else there—became aware that this was another holographic image, like the one of General Hawk back at the battle site.

"Gentlemen," Hawk said to Duke and Rip, "this is Mr. James McCullen of MARS Industries, the visionary who built the warheads you've so diligently guarded."

Cameras positioned all around the Control Room were even now sending images of the G.I. JOE team (and Duke and Rip) back to McCullen's HQ, where in a small chamber he stood with their holographic images all around him.

"General," McCullen said, in a smooth baritone, "most men I've encountered in this business over-promise and under-deliver. You, on the other hand, are quite the opposite—clearly, you were right and I was wrong. You were the security option I *should* have chosen."

Behind his cool military demeanor, Duke was steaming. He said, "My team did everything we could out there. A lot of good people were lost—"

"But not *you*, Captain," McCullen said, a cold edge in his voice.

"That mission, sir," Duke replied, "was classified. *Clearly*, somebody sold us out."

McCullen said, "I have spent ten years and thirteen billion Euros creating these four warheads. Your job, Captain, was to protect them for less than one day . . . and if it hadn't been for the initiative of General Hawk here, you would have *failed*."

Hawk cut in: "That's not a fair assessment, Mr. McCullen. The captain followed his orders to the letter."

"Well, that wasn't enough, was it?"

Duke bristled, but said nothing.

McCullen's holo-image turned to Hawk. "What are your coordinates? I'll have NATO send another Special Ops team to retrieve the warheads— company strength, this time."

"With apologies, Mr. McCullen, and with all due respect—it's not that I don't trust *you,* it's that I don't trust *anybody.*"

McCullen only smiled at that. "Are sure you don't have McCullen blood in you, General?"

The general returned the smile. "I don't talk smooth enough to be a McCullen, I'm afraid."

"Seems to me, General, you do just fine. Now . . . so that the bastards who attacked you can't find you, you need to disable the tracking beacon in that case."

"We already have."

"Good," McCullen said. "Good. So . . . can I count on you to deliver the warheads to NATO now?"

Hawk shook his head. "I think it's unwise to expose them at the moment. This hostile group might make another attempt. We need to find them, and neutralize them, before we can consider moving your weapons."

McCullen was nodding. "All right. But surely

you'll allow me to check the warheads to see if any have been damaged?"

Hawk gave Duke a look, and Duke—begrudgingly—set down the hardshell case.

Breaker turned his eyepiece to X-Ray mode, and revealed the nano-mites crawling around inside the four warheads like countless insects.

McCullen said, "Open the case, please."

Breaker said, "Sir, my scan indicates they are intact. . . ."

McCullen's holo-image turned to Hawk. "General?"

Hawk said, "What's the code?"

Duke listened carefully as McCullen gave it up: "Five-two-nine-four-four-oh."

Breaker keyed in the code.

As the case opened, Breaker discreetly watched McCullen as the holo-image's fingers ran over the warheads.

Satisfied, their holographic guest turned to Hawk again. "Please do keep me informed of your progress, General."

McCullen shot the briefest glare Duke's way; but not so brief that Duke wasn't able to return it. . . .

Then, the feed cut, McCullen was gone, as if a TV remote had switched him off.

Scarlett's eyes were on Breaker, whose expression betrayed concern. "Breaker? What is it?"

Breaker said, "My voice analyzer on our guest was going up, and down, and sideways. On some level, for some reason, he was jamming us."

Heavy Duty said, "The guy is working an angle he doesn't want us to catch."

Rip asked, "Whose side is he *on,* anyway?"

No one responded; but all of their faces revealed how seriously they took that question.

CHAPTER FIVE
A Truly Magnificent Creature

Gliding through deep Arctic Ocean, below polar ice caps, the sleekly modern submarine—a next-generation variation on a Trident—bore the symbol of no nation. Though the craft's capacity as an instrument of destruction should not be underestimated, the sub served primarily as a mobile headquarters for the CEO of MARS Industries, whose logo the ship displayed.

And right now that CEO, James McCullen, remained within the darkened holo-projection chamber, his meeting with General Hawk and his people now over.

But McCullen did not step off the small platform, as another hologram—a quite lovely one—shimmered into view at another holo station.

Still in her skintight black body armor, the beautiful brunette known to some as the Baroness stood with hands on hips, and with an expression of open displeasure.

McCullen, without yet looking at her, knew that

she was there (or that is, that her hologram was there); and he also anticipated her unhappiness.

He shared it.

"I have spent the last five years," he said with a curl of his upper lip, "putting all of this into motion . . . wringing money out of NATO, planning every chess move, searching out every contingency. This was supposed to be the *easy* part."

"If," Ana said tightly, "you had let me stage the assault at your precious factory, and not on the open road, we could have contained the situation."

He turned toward the image. "What, and lose the trust of our clients in the process? No, the loss of the warheads had to rest clearly at NATO's feet."

Her eyes flared. "You *knew* the G.I. JOE group might get involved. Abernathy himself approached you!"

"I thought I'd deflected him—and I obviously thought wrong. But you knew, as well, of the possibility of the JOEs engaging us; that's why we assembled so strong, so large an assault team."

"Not strong enough," she said, shaking her head. "Not large enough."

McCullen stared with unvarnished suspicion at his beautiful associate. "What happened to you, anyway? You had the weapons case in your hands! Was it *him*? Was it because *he* was there? Did you hesitate when—"

"It had nothing to do with Hauser," she said crisply. "And everything to do with the JOEs."

McCullen's expression, his manner, softened. "Forgive me, my dear. Handling jealousy is not my strong suit."

She ignored that. "Have you tracked the weapons case?"

He twitched a half-smile. "G.I. JOE deactivated the homing beacon, of course . . . but I gave them a code that *re*activated it, without their knowledge."

McCullen leaned over to a control panel, hit a key, and a monitor screen materialized, displaying a map of the world, a beacon light flashing over a spot in the Egyptian desert, grid coordinates blinking.

"And here we have it," McCullen said softly, smiling fully now, "the exact location of a secret command center, only mentioned in whispers. . . . Who holds the top hand *now*, my dear?"

She was smiling, as well, though it was a bitter, self-confident one. "I *will* get those warheads back. You can count on it."

He stepped forward and lovingly caressed the face that wasn't really there, his fingers slipping right through the "flesh" of the image.

His whisper was a bizarre mix of tenderness and menace as he said, "I *am* counting on you, my dear. I am."

She flipped her hair, diffusing the threat, saying, "If I were really there? I *might* actually let you touch me."

His smile turning sly, McCullen said, "I could send a jet. . . ."

"Business first," she said. "Anyway, I'm a married woman . . . remember?"

He was still smiling when her holo-form blinked off.

From behind him came a familiar male voice, its accent distinctly Japanese: "If you had sent me, the job would be done now."

McCullen turned as a figure in white stepped up to him—the agent known only as Storm Shadow. The hood the ninja (Arishikage Clan) wore into battle was off, but otherwise the long white jacket, with its turned-up collar, and matching breeches and boots, indicated Storm Shadow was ready to fight. So did the hilts of the two swords poking up from sheaths on his back.

And the throwing star the ninja tossed playfully in his fingers, like an oldtime gangster flipping a coin, was nothing to be taken lightly.

McCullen knew that some day the ninja's excessive confidence and pride, which at times could emerge as near insolence, might get the man in trouble. Storm Shadow's saving grace, however, was his inherent sense of honor.

"Whether I should have chosen you in the first place," McCullen said, "is a moot point. What is important is that I'm sending you now. There's no room for any more mistakes. The schedule must not be compromised any further."

"Understood."

McCullen started off, then paused and turned

back and added: "Keep an eye on the Baroness for me—"

But no one was there.

Storm Shadow had already gone, like the ghost his white apparel suggested, with only the throwing star—spinning on the floor—to indicate he hadn't been just another hologram.

Moving from the hologram chamber into the adjacent office, McCullen found Zartan, his aide-de-camp, lounging in a yellow chair in the sleekly deco suite, seated at a table arrayed with fruit, a water bottle on ice, and a selection of books on the American form of government, from McCullen's own voluminous library. Zartan was reading one of these, and several others were cracked open to save his place.

The broad-shouldered, dark-haired aide in the black shirt and slacks seemed physically wrong for such intellectual pursuits; but his handsome, oval face with its sharp eyes and perpetually amused mouth, indicated keen intelligence.

Only McCullen knew that this was homework of a sort, for a mission so secret only he and Zartan knew it was in progress. . . .

The master of the submarine went to a large oval Perspex window and had a look out at the frigid ocean. They were approaching the huge docking bay of a massive facility built into the seabed under the jagged canopy of the polar ice cap, an underwater fortress defended by numerous harpoon guns and a fearsome turbo-pulse cannon.

To a visitor, this would be a breathtaking, even frightening, vista. And even to McCullen, its majesty was not lost—seeing what his mind and his money were creating exhilarated him. . . .

In the flight control room of the underwater base, technicians were working at computer consoles. Through the Perspex windows, they could see outside where the giant docking bay door was closing behind the submarine as it glided into the facility's docking area.

Soon McCullen was on the dry land of the bay, and activity was everywhere. The enormous facility was still being built, workers using high-tech blowtorches to solder steel beams, others conveying materials via vehicles with MARS logos, the bustling surroundings giving McCullen a real boost after the disappointments of the day.

Few things startled him, but having a glass case on a cart wheeled up in front of him by a figure, blocking his way, certainly did—especially when that glass case held a hissing king cobra. . . .

Much could be said about the man called simply the Doctor, but a mastery of social skills was not among them. Still, McCullen could not fault the poor devil, whose life-support mask—a tubular device of the Doctor's own invention—covered the lower half of his face, his nose included, like a pilot's air supply, continually pumping air into his lungs while mechanically helping him speak despite his damaged vocal chords. The finishing touch was the dark-blue monocle that concealed his left eye.

Apart from the bizarre visage, the Doctor presented himself well enough—a gray tailored coat, dark trousers and boots, all vaguely British in cut—though his dark hair was a long, tangled mass.

Lord Byron as mad scientist, McCullen thought.

"A magnificent creature, the king cobra," the Doctor rasped mechanically, as he gestured with a black-gloved hand. "Don't you agree, Mr. McCullen?"

What could be seen of the Doctor's face indicated a man perhaps only in his twenties, but the mind behind that Halloween facial gizmo was the best that money could buy. McCullen's money.

"Mother Nature's grim reaper," the Doctor said fondly, his voice a ghastly breathy, halting thing. He was gesturing to the snake like a used car salesman indicating a particularly nice, low-mileage model. "Her symbol of lethal purpose . . . unseen until it strikes, the king cobra's venom can kill a fully grown elephant . . . with a single bite."

"Charming," McCullen said. "I could not have hoped for a warmer homecoming."

"I have a much better welcoming gift." He gestured nearby to a holding area taken up by a group of twenty barefoot men in black T-shirts and trousers, reflecting various ethnicities, but all with formidable physical builds. They all stood at attention, not a single muscle moving among them, each with less expression than a store-window manikin.

"I am calling them Neo-Vipers, Mr. McCullen," the Doctor's raspy, artificial voice proudly intoned.

"Not just Vipers?"

"No. Significant improvements have been made. As you can see, we've been very busy while you were away."

"But have you been *successful*?"

"We have made strides. Come with me, please."

McCullen followed the Doctor to the men, who stood at stony attention. The Doctor stepped up to the nearest one and lifted an ear lobe with a finger, revealing an incision scar.

"We injected one thousand cc's of the nano-mite solution into each subject," the Doctor said.

From his coat pocket, the Doctor withdrew a handheld computer and pressed a few keys, producing on the screen a file photo of a random subject.

"What am I looking at, Doctor?"

He pointed to an information window. "Their brain scans show complete inactivity in the self-preservation region of the cortex . . . when they finally stopped screaming, that is."

"Self-preservation region of the cortex? Layman's terms, Doctor. In English, please?"

The Doctor shrugged. "Put it this way: *They feel no fear.*"

He keyed in a command on the handheld, and the subject on the screen stepped from among the

Neo-Vipers and came forward and held his bare
arm out . . .

. . . and through a portal into the glass case that
held the waiting cobra.

Matter of factly, the Doctor commented: "Corti-
cal nerve clusters reveal complete inactivity—"

"Doctor," McCullen said. There were workers
all around, and this cruelty—however it might be
justified by scientific research—would hardly be
good for morale.

But, as the cobra reared into its familiar warning
posture, its head flattening out as the creature eyed
the intruding forearm, the Doctor merely continued in his clinical rasp: "These subjects *feel* no
pain."

Suddenly the subject's hand grabbed the cobra
about midway, and the snake responded by biting
the man's arm, latching onto it, sinking its ven-
omous fangs into a prominent vein.

And the dead-eyed subject didn't even wince.

"In addition," the Doctor said, as if showing
McCullen around a garden and pointing out interesting flora, "frontal lobe concepts of morality are
disengaged. And this, Mr. MuCullen, means *no*
sense of *remorse*. . . ."

With another deftly keyed-in command from the
Doctor, the subject obediently let loose of the snake
and slipped his arm out of the glass case, only to
stand at continued attention, as if nothing at all
had happened, and as if the terrible red marks on
his arm were not there.

McCullen, frowning with interest, asked, "And these subjects are utterly obedient?"

"Of course," the Doctor said casually. "And the real world applications? Virtually endless."

The subject's knees gave out, and McCullen watched with a clinical curiosity worthy of the Doctor, as the Neo-Viper's bite wound revealed the bubbling of activity.

What McCullen could sense, but not see, were the thousands of microscopic nano-mites rushing—as venom raced through a labyrinth of veins—to take that deadly venom, head on, first blocking it, then pushing it back, all the way to the original fang punctures.

McCullen watched in astonishment as the venom seeped harmlessly out of the puncture wounds, dripping off the subject's arm like rainwater.

The subject got to his feet and returned to his place in line with his silent brethren, back at attention.

The Doctor's smile could not be seen, due to the breathing apparatus; but McCullen could sense it as the scientist said, "So you tell me, sir—would you say is it working? Have we, or have we not, made strides?"

McCullen nodded. "I am favorably impressed, Doctor. Very favorably impressed."

"Nothing could please me more than hearing you say that."

With a curt nod of dismissal, McCullen said,

"Send a team of your 'Neo-Vipers' to rendezvous with Storm Shadow and the Baroness."

Soon McCullen was moving quickly through the ultramodern corridors of his underwater base; but then, to his mild irritation, he realized the Doctor was tagging along.

"We already have the prototype unit in place," the Doctor was saying, almost giddily. "We have a single subject who is *perfect*."

"You've done well," McCullen said, almost offhandedly. "You've thrown the caber clear out of the yard."

He referred to a test of strength among Scottish youth, who would attempt to throw a tree trunk, a caber, a manful distance.

"Thank you, sir," the Doctor said, working to keep up. "But there is so much more research that needs to be done. Might I make one small suggestion?"

McCullen stopped and glanced behind him at the eager puppy in the strange steel-and-rubber mask.

"Selling just one batch of warheads to the black market," the Doctor began, "could fund my complete research program, and—"

"I appreciate your thirst for knowledge, Doctor. It's certainly . . . admirable. But this world is messy enough already." He shook his head, firmly. "No. What the world needs right now, at this crucial moment in history, is unification. Strong, firm leadership. This world cries out to be taken out of chaos by someone willing to take *complete* control."

McCullen glanced at a portal nearby, into an operating chamber, where his aide Zartan stood whistling as he was scanned by robotic attendants. A monitor screen revealed what the process would be: *Zartan's fingerprints were being changed.* A small first step in Zartan's aspect of McCullen's master plan.

Something wistful came into the MARS CEO's voice as he said, "My ancestors were once very close indeed to performing this role, the role of saviors to a troubled world." He laughed but it was bitter. "If it hadn't been for the damn *French*. . . . Ironic that the biggest cowards on earth, the world's chronic surrender merchants, should be the ones who stood in our way."

Zartan noticed his leader watching him through the portal and gave him a nod, cracking his knuckles as if in indication of the job ahead.

McCullen said to the scientist, "When I finish what I have put in motion, Doctor, the money will take care of itself . . . and you will be able to do all of the research you desire. With my full support and blessing. . . . Now, if you'll excuse me."

And McCullen strode off, past a worker soldering a steel beam with a high-tech blowtorch.

The Doctor stared after him, his reaction to McCullen's words a mystery behind the mask.

CHAPTER SIX

The Promise

The image on the monitor at a console station in the Control Room of the Pit was all too familiar to Duke Hauser. But he managed to maintain his game face; at least, he thought so . . . yet there she was, Ana, the woman of his dreams, and nightmares. . . .

Breaker explained, "That's the best of the images we grabbed during the firefight."

Ripcord, however, had lost his game face, and then some; it had melted and dripped off his mug until nothing was left behind but a stunned expression worthy of a clubbed baby seal.

He leaned closer to Duke and whispered, "Hey, man . . . isn't that—"

Duke cut his friend off with a sharp look.

Breaker, at the console keyboard, was producing a fully three-dimensional front view of the warrior woman's lovely face.

Duke watched with a sick feeling as the slender communications expert's fingers flew and, on the adjacent monitor, a series of photos of females began to appear and disappear, endlessly, as the computer did its thing.

"These days," Breaker said, "we can run a face through an infinity scan."

The stunningly beautiful aide called Cover Girl leaned in. "We have access to any photograph on any server anywhere in the world."

Breaker shrugged. "Everybody gets photographed in some way at some time—ATM machines, airports, crowd shots at sporting events."

From behind them came General Hawk's quietly commanding voice: "We'll find her. Then we'll work our way up the chain, and find whoever sent her."

Duke was frozen, watching with inner horror as Ana's face stared at him even as thousands of other women's vaguely similar faces whizzed by on the adjacent screen.

Rip put a hand on his friend's shoulder and whispered gently, "Bro . . . you okay?"

"Rip," he muttered, anything but okay, "what the hell *happened* to her?"

For once in his life, Rip didn't seem to know what to say.

From the smart tablet in her hand, a beep alerted Cover Girl, who handed the small computer to the general, saying, "From NATO, sir."

His eyes quickly took in the small screen. "I am now the official custodian of those warheads." He looked up at Duke and gave him a tight smile. "Captain, your mission is complete."

But Duke's nod had a hint of defeat in it. "Sir, when you move it, she"—he nodded toward Ana on the screen—"she and her people are going to come at you with everything they have . . . and that would seem to be a lot. You know that, right?"

"Certainly, son."

"And with her intel, and her boys, and her toys . . . she'll find you. Maybe she'll find you *first*. . . ."

Hawk was frowning, not a deep frown, but a frown nonetheless. "Your point being . . . ?"

"You can't let that happen. You *have* to get to her first. You have to go after her right now."

"No disagreement here."

"Good. Because I want in."

Rip, at Duke's side, said, "Let us *both* in on this, sir. Our team just got wasted. I think we deserve a little consideration, here. A little payback."

Hawk's eyes remained cold. "You don't get to ask to be a part of G.I. JOE. You *get* asked."

Duke stepped forward. "Didn't you say you scouted me four years ago? Maybe you didn't think I was ready, then. Well, I'm ready now. Let's have at these bastards."

Hawk's face softened. "Look, Captain . . . I know all about losing men. Good men. Nothing hurts more. But attempting to—"

"I *know* her," Duke said.

Rip winced, as if he'd been slapped.

The general didn't seem to think he'd heard right. "Excuse me?" he said.

Duke led with his chin. "General Hawk, you said knowing is half the battle. Well, I know who she is."

For several long seconds, no one spoke.

Then Hawk said, "You can't blackmail your way onto this team, soldier."

"I don't intend to try."

Duke reached into a pocket and withdrew a snapshot, which he showed to the general—a photo of the woman who had led the attack on the convoy, but in kinder days, four years before, a softer-looking beauty—blonde, not brunette, blue-eyed, not brown—staring lovingly at Duke as they were about to kiss.

"Her name is Ana Lewis," Duke said, very businesslike, "and I can tell you everything you need to know about her. Or anyway, I can do that up till four years ago. After that, well . . . obviously a lot's changed."

"And more than her hair color," Rip put in.

Hawk was not easily surprised; but right now his eyes traveled from the photo to Duke and back again, staring in disbelief.

"You and I need to talk, Captain," Hawk said.

And Duke followed the man from the Pit into a masculine, unpretentious office that appeared to be part of the general's stateroom, with his living quarters attached. Though there were the requisite trophies here and there, and framed citations, awards and photographs on the wall, these were spartan digs.

There was also a heavy safe, a small bank vault, built into the wall of the stateroom, in the corner off the general's desk.

Duke waited for General Hawk to seat himself behind the desk, then took the chair opposite.

Hawk was saying, "Before this goes any further, I need to know what . . . or *who* . . . I'm dealing with."

"As I said, her name is Ana Lewis, General, and—"

"I don't mean the woman—I mean *you*, Captain. I need to know if I'm dealing a man who can put mission first. Or are you a man just looking to settle a score? Because I don't have to tell you . . . but I will, anyway . . . that the battlefield is the wrong place for such emotional baggage. For example . . . *could you kill her?*"

Without hesitation, Duke said, "If I had to."

"Well, that's good . . . because chances are, you *will* have to." Hawk shifted in his swivel chair. "But if you flinch even for just an instant, and this I promise you . . . she will kill *you*. This much we know, having seen the woman in combat."

"I'm well aware, sir."

Hawk grimaced, his eyes turning to slits. "What I'm trying to say, soldier, is that unless you can kill her *graveyard* dead, I don't want you."

"I can do that," Duke said flatly.

But the general's expression retained its skepticism, and Duke continued: "I signed on to deliver those warheads. And, sir? I intend to finish the job."

Hawk studied the young man for what seemed forever, and was perhaps ten seconds.

"So," Hawk said, finally, casually. "Tell me about her."

"Okay. But first things first . . . is this room secure?"

"As secure as they come."

"Good. Because this is between you and me, sir."

Four years before, more or less, in Washington, D.C., the dance floor of a certain military club was crowded, both officers and enlisted men and women with their spouses or dates having a wonderful evening dancing to somewhat old-fashioned music from a live orchestra.

Many beautiful women were present, but the most beautiful, to Duke Hauser, was easily Ana Lewis, a slender, shapely blonde in a formfitting black dress. Four years from now, she would display a certain cold viciousness on an attack on a convoy; but on this balmy evening, she appeared only young and warm and lovely.

Lieutenant Hauser had fallen prey to the love-at-first-sight cliché with Ana, and he was a guy who'd gotten around and wasn't prone to such foolishness. But he did love her, and she, miracle of miracles, seemed to love him. At the moment, they were dancing to a romantic ballad, pressed to each other with familiar intimacy.

He whispered to her: "That looks a little ambitious even for Rip, don't you think?"

She glanced over at Ripcord, at a floorside table, downing shots with a quartet of enlisted women.

She laughed. "Let's not tell him that the one next to him is General Murphy's daughter."

Duke laughed back. "Let's not."

As they danced by his booth, they could hear Rip saying, "Ladies, my hot tub holds four, easy. . . . *Five* with a little effort."

They were still laughing at that when Duke led Ana outside onto a quiet verandah, where a handful of tables awaited them, couples seated romantically here and there, but one table was free, and they took it. The lights of Washington shimmered beyond them as if a jewel box had been emptied into the night.

Speaking of jewels. . . .

Suddenly, dramatically, he knelt before her like a knight to his lady. He displayed the small box in his hand, open to reveal the very respectably-sized diamond engagement ring—this was a mission he had carefully planned and was now flawlessly executing.

Ana gasped with shock and joy, her eyes as bright as the diamond she was regarding.

Shyly, he said, "I've been wanting to do this before we deploy."

"Duke . . . it's beautiful. It's *too* nice, you wonderful lunatic."

He slipped back into his chair, and said, "Only

time I'll ever be buyin' one of these, so why not splurge a little?"

They stared into each other's faces, and the moment was a lovely one . . . at least until Duke realized he hadn't actually gotten an answer out of her yet.

"Well, baby. . . . What do you say?"

She was trying to say something, but her emotions were clogging the way.

From behind them they heard a very familiar voice say: "Say *yes*, you idiot girl. Don't you know a real American hero when you see one?"

Ana's older brother, Rex, sauntered up, looking spiffy in his pressed Army uniform with its medical insignia on the collar. He was boyishly handsome with an infectious smile, and his expression conveyed instantly how happy he was for them.

Kneeling by their table, with one hand on Duke's shoulder and the other on his sister's, Rex said, "You better say yes, before I spill the state secrets to my prospective brother-in-law . . . such as what it's like to share a damn *bathroom* with you."

"Rex," Duke said, with a grin, "you do know how to kill a mood."

"Sorry, buddy. I was just coming over to offer you a ride back to the post."

Ana frowned. "It's that time already?"

Duke half-smiled. "We go at oh-five-hundred."

"Is it . . . ?" She frowned. "It *is*, right? You're going. That's why you're pulling Rex out of the lab to—"

"Ana," Duke said, "you know we can't say—"

"Yes, I know, yes, yes. Classified. Top Secret. You'd have to kill me if you told me, blah, blah, blah."

Duke chuckled. "Well, speaking of classified information. . . . You still haven't given me an answer."

"Yes!" The big blue eyes popped. "*Of course,* it's yes."

He let out a relieved sigh, but the tip of her forefinger came to his lips.

"One condition, big boy. . . ."

She grabbed Rex and pulled him over. "Promise me you won't let my genius brother get hurt." Her eyes went to Rex, and the love there was unmistakable. "This little egghead is the only family I have left." And now her eyes traveled to her fiancé. "*Promise* me. . . ."

"I promise," he said.

Her smile was a trembling thing, a leaf in a breeze, as she held out her hand and allowed him to thread the ring onto the proper finger.

Rex took this in with a smile, though his eyes hinted at the loss he felt, his sister's love promised to another man. . . .

Behind them came a shatter of glass, and a figure crashed to the brick floor of the verandah, near the trio—Rip, arms and legs akimbo, had joined the little group.

Duke said, "Jesus, Rip! Are you making an entrance or an exit?"

Rip ignored this, checking his jaw to see if it still worked after the blow he'd received that had sent him flying onto the verandah.

He yelled back into the main room: "Your damn *hand* is gonna *feel* that, in the morning!"

Still on the floor, Rip glanced up at his friends, nodded hello, then noticed the ritual in progress. "Hey, man, nice rock! You finally proposing to this girl?"

"I'm done proposing," Duke said.

"And I already said yes," Ana said.

"Well," Rip said, "it ain't official till you answer *my* question. Do you love my main man?"

"With all my heart. Always and forever."

That was when Rip got out his cellphone and snapped the picture that, four years later, Duke would share with General Hawk.

But at the moment, all Rip could do was study the photo of the loving couple with longing.

"Looks like now I've gotta find somebody to love me . . ." He got up and headed back in. ". . . starting in my hot tub, and for as many times as possible in the next three hours. . . ."

Duke, Ana, and Rip shared laughter at their irascible friend, unaware that they would never again have another moment together of such happiness.

As Duke Hauser shared the love story gone wrong with General Hawk, the object of the young captain's conflicted emotions was in France—specifically, Paris, where she lived in a château with the man she had married, a man who was definitely not the lieutenant who had proposed to her on bended knee at a military club, four years before.

She swooped into her mansion, peeling off her fur coat over a wispy gown and depositing the coat in the arms of a waiting servant.

Also waiting was her husband, Baron Leon De-Cobray, who approached her with mild impatience.

"Finally," he said. He wore a smoking jacket and a weary mantle of sophistication. "You're home."

"Good evening, Leon. How was your meeting with the Minister of Defense?"

His eyebrows flicked upward, her question momentarily distracting him. "He was thrilled. We *all* were—the accelerator performed flawlessly. I do wish you could have been there."

She began striding up the endless staircase without him. "Yes, you and your little lab rats are so very clever."

He started up after her, his effort to contain his anger very apparent to her, even with her back to him.

"How was Monte Carlo?" he asked.

"Disappointing," she said. "I did not get what I was after."

"Perhaps I should be grateful."

"Most husbands would be."

Closer now, just behind her, holding his temper a lost cause now, he said, "Most husbands don't have such mysterious wives. Most husbands know exactly where their women *are*, and what their women *do*."

"I'm no one's 'woman,' darling . . . and anyway, they only *think* they know. . . ."

In the master bedroom, Ana threw open the double doors on the highest floor of the château and helped herself to the magnificent view of the City of Lights, with the Eiffel Tower positioned postcard perfect in the vista.

She heard her husband coming in, and turned that way, catching a glimpse of a figure in the anteroom to the left of the door. Her husband was coming quickly over to her, unaware they had a guest.

That guest was a figure in startling white—McCullen's ninja, Storm Shadow.

Decobray was saying, "Ana, darling, I don't want us to argue. I *missed* you, my dear."

She drew him close and kissed him. Even with her husband's lips on hers, she could see Storm Shadow making a move toward them. When her husband fell into an almost pitiful embrace, she managed to warn the ninja away with her eyes.

She looked at Decobray, summoning an expression that suggested fondness. "Let me freshen up, darling, and I'll join you downstairs."

Placated, the smitten man smiled and nodded, saying, "I do love you, my beautiful Baroness. I do love you."

"I know," she said.

He took his leave.

Then Ana spun around and headed straight for

her uninvited guest, who stood nodding toward where the husband had disappeared. The ninja's hood was off, his black hair brushing his forehead in studied nonchalance, the contempt in his expression clear.

"McCullen gave me orders to kill your precious Baron," Storm Shadow said, "if he so much as touches you."

Her eyes flared. "*Of course,* he touches me, you fool. He's my *husband.* Besides, his work at the lab goes much better after we've . . . touched. And isn't that the important thing?"

The ninja said nothing. He specialized in tactics, not the overview.

"So," she said regally, "do you mind tell me what the hell you're doing here, in my bedroom? Spying on me, are you?"

She hardly saw him draw the katana blade that flashed past her face.

"If I was spying on you," he said, "you would never know it."

She showed him a spooked look, but it was only to cover the knife she brought up, hoping to get the point right up to his nearest eye; but he grabbed her wrist, and stopped it an inch away.

"You have to admit," she said with a smile, "I'm getting closer."

Storm Shadow granted her a rare smile. "You always were my best student."

Both lowered their blades.

"I'll be coming with you," he said.

"With me?"

"To retrieve the warheads. McCullen's command."

"All right."

In Japanese, he said, *"We go at dawn."*

She nodded.

Storm Shadow turned and went out a side door.

Then the mistress of the mansion walked to an antique dresser worth the price of a Bentley and opened a drawer, and then opened another drawer, a smaller, hidden one.

Within was a tiny box.

Without taking it from the drawer, she gently opened the box and revealed the diamond engagement ring, which winked at her knowingly.

For a few moments, she studied the stone, with sad and lonely eyes, recalling a balmy night in D.C. four years before.

And then she threw water on her face, touched up her makeup, changed into a nightgown, and went down to deal with her damn husband.

CHAPTER SEVEN
Learning
Experience

Yesterday, riding with General Hawk down from the landing platform to the Control Room of the Pit, Duke and Ripcord had glimpsed a training area at which they were getting an up-close-and-personal look today.

The Urban Combat Center was a vast space utilized as an indoor variation on Hogan's Alley, the FBI Academy's tactical training facility. On all sides were the geometric shapes of gray faceless, bullet-pocked concrete that were the mock buildings of Any Big City, USA, with glass-less windows for hologram foes to take shots at those training in the open space below. Here and there, LED readouts kept track of the trainees' progress (or lack thereof), and metal catwalks joined the two sides of the imaginary, entirely blank street.

Right now, Heavy Duty—in a black T-shirt and camo-trousers—was saying to Duke and Rip (at parade rest nearby), "Far as I'm concerned, you two blackmailed your way onto this damn team."

That wasn't how Duke saw it, or Rip for that

matter, but both were soldiers who knew not to enter into such discussions with an officer training them.

"Doesn't mean I've gotta *like* it," Heavy Duty continued, getting something out of a metal case, "but it does mean I've gotta get you birds mission-ready—JOE style. This is the Delta Six Accelerator Suit."

To Duke, the bunch of silver-metallic parts looked like high-tech football pads.

Rip asked, "What's it accelerate?"

"*You,*" Heavy Duty said. "It'll make you run faster, jump higher, and hit harder than any enemy."

Having seen those skull-helmeted soldiers Ana had been hanging out with, Duke had his doubts; but he said nothing.

Then a titanium boot was sliding over a shoe, after which cobalt machine parts were snapping into place over Rip's arms and legs, with a mechanical hiss.

"Head-to-toe turbo-hydraulics," Heavy Duty explained, "highly pressurized pneumatics."

Duke, who could follow that, and Rip, who didn't, both snapped on aerodynamic, flying-wing helmets, within which a powering-up produced an ear-piercing whine that had both men wincing, but briefly. Laser-enhanced LED readouts scrambled and fritzed across the Heads-Up-Displays of their plexi visors.

"You will note," Heavy Duty said, as matter-of-fact as a weatherman predicting rain, "the advanced cybernetics HUD being fed into your helmets."

Duke was checking out the two spears and five wrist-rockets at his left forearm.

Heavy Duty picked up on that: "Twin gas-propelled grappling spears. Five twenty-millimeter, high-explosive, heat-seeking, fire-and-forget rockets."

Rip was spinning the barrels of a Gatling-type submachine gun on his right forearm. He was grinning like a kid Christmas morning who Santa brought a really special toy.

"That's my personal favorite," Heavy Duty admitted to Rip, nodding at the submachine gun. "A ten-millimeter, caseless submachine gun, capable of firing fifty rounds per second. Fully self-contained firepower. Perfect for a couple of cowboys like you two."

Duke and Rip were buckled in now, getting a feel for the flexible, poly-alloy suits, well aware that they now looked more like robots than men.

Rip asked, "You mind repeating that?"

Heavy Duty frowned. "Repeating what?"

"Everything. I may have missed a couple points—got distracted by how cool I look." He turned to his pal. "What do you say, Duke? Pretty damn cool, huh?"

Duke ignored that and, thankfully, so did Heavy

Duty, who gave them a long-suffering look, then asked, "Any *real* questions?"

Rip said, "Just one."

Heavy Duty's eyes narrowed. "What's that?"

"How do you go to the bathroom in this thing?"

"Feel free to go right in the suit."

"Yeah?"

"It will probably electrocute you, but feel free."

Duke smiled at that, but Rip was frowning, thinking it over.

Soon Duke and Rip were out of the suits and ready for some real training. They wore light body armor up top and camo-trousers below, were heavily armed and ready to rock and roll. First things first was an obstacle course set up in the Hogan's Alley that required dexterity even without the bad guys in windows popping up to sometimes shoot at you.

They were still on the obstacle course, battling hologram terrorists in windows and doorways, when a cool, sleek Spyder Attack vehicle hurtled up to the edge of the urban combat area.

The JOE behind the wheel was a muscular soldier who had clearly been around many a block, likely leaving considerable damage in his wake. In a beret, combat vest, camo-trousers and boots, he looked ready to go to war, as he hopped down from the vehicle.

This was Lieutenant Stone, tall, rugged, with clipped brown hair, blue eyes and a firm jaw—a specialist in recon and jungle warfare, not to mention hand-to-hand combat.

He nodded a greeting to Heavy Duty—currently armed with a clipboard and pen—and looked toward the obstacle course, where Duke and Rip were hustling out of an area draped with smoke, the two longtime buddies bumping fists at their successful run.

Stone asked, "New JOEs?"

"Hell no."

"Then what are they doing here?"

"Long story."

Stone didn't ask what it was.

Scarlett was among the observers, and right now Rip was waiting for the buzzer that signaled when he was to enter the next leg of the course; he took the opportunity to throw a wink Scarlett's way.

"Just so you know?" he said genially. "When I want something, when I get a target in my sights? . . . I take it *down*. . . ."

"Just so you know?" she said with a lovely, acid smile.

"I don't impress easily."

The buzzer buzzed and Rip charged forward, firing up at various hologram terrorists in windows, who were shooting back at him. He felt good, even without Duke at his side; just *knew* he was tearing it up, he was in the damn *zone*. . . .

Duke had been peeled off by Heavy Duty for another phase of training. His overall scores were so high, Heavy D had decided to move him along, and was now handing him body armor and helmet.

"What's this for?" Duke asked.

"Let's just say you're gonna need it. . . ."

This proved to be an understatement. He found himself facing the masked ninja in black, Snake Eyes, in a two-man tourney witnessed by twenty or more JOEs. Both combatants had silver-tipped black variations on the military's bayonet training tool, the Pugil stick. These, like everything at this damn place, were "next-gen"—the little blue flashing lights along the plump tips indicated as much to Duke.

But a stick was a stick . . . was a stick. Wasn't it?

The answer: No. Not when that stick was in the hands of a martial arts expert like Snake Eyes; and not when that stick conveyed a stunning electrical charge. . . .

Duke had blocked half a dozen blows before Snake Eyes sent him down on the concrete floor, or anyway the all-too-thin rubber pad there, where he could see as well as feel the crackling electrical shock rippling across his armor and through his body.

The savvy-looking older soldier called Stone was their referee, and his seasoned eyes watched, motioning Snake Eyes back, as Duke—feeling winded—still determinedly got to his feet, Pugil stick in his grasp.

"Let's try that," Duke said, "again."

Stone smiled a little, though Heavy Duty just

watched impassively, his face having no more expression than the massive biceps exposed by his sleeveless T-shirt.

Elsewhere, Rip had just gotten blown off his feet by a terrorist. How those holograms could pack such firepower he would never understand. Hauling himself up, he noticed Scarlett—clipboard in one hand, her other hand scribbling furiously—gliding by him.

"I thought you took down everything that got in your sights?" she asked coolly. "Guess maybe you don't want me that bad . . . do you, Rip?"

He wanted her, all right; and he made no attempt to wipe the helpless, smitten expression off his puss.

That expression was noted by another observer, Breaker, casually having his lunch, a microwaved burrito. He paused to check something in his eyepiece.

"Awww," Breaker said. "Ain't that sweet."

Rip scowled at him. "*What* is?"

"Your little heart just skipped a beat."

The scowl turned into a full-bore sneer.

Meanwhile, Duke—who'd been down several more times—was fighting valiantly against Snake Eyes, who seemed to Duke a solid candidate for World's Greatest Ninja about now.

Once again he hit the floor, hard, crackling with electricity, wincing in pain.

Stone held up a hand, saying, "That's it, gents. Fight's over. . . ."

The ref walked away, heading over to the watching Heavy Duty, and didn't see at first that Duke had ignored him calling the fight, and was back on his feet again.

"*Again,*" Duke demanded of Snake Eyes.

Snake Eyes nodded assent.

Stone was smirking and his eyes were wide. He said to Heavy Duty, "You *sure* that one's not a JOE?"

Finally, Heavy Duty—standing with his massive arms folded, his note-taking forgotten—betrayed in his dark eyes at least a touch of admiration for the non-JOE's spirit, anyway.

Back in Hogan's Alley, Rip was diving and rolling, and firing away, "killing" the last two terrorists, just before the sixty-second buzzer sounded. Around him the floor was littered with hologram bad guys, one of whom was only wounded but out of action.

Weapon in one hand, other hand on his hip, Rip grinned in unashamed self-worth, a big fat cocky grin he shared with Scarlett, who was doing her best not to look impressed.

"You left one alive," she told him.

He bounded up to her, saying, "Gimme a break, girl! That has *gotta* be some kind of *record.*"

"The record is twenty."

"Out of twenty."

"That's right."

"I shot twenty."

"You shot nineteen. Wounded one."

He smirked. "Let me guess—record holder is that Snake Eyes cat, right?"

"No."

"*Who*, then?"

"Me. Piece of friendly advice? If you're going to shoot at something, *kill* it—otherwise, take up knitting."

She walked off before he could see her mischievous smile. Passing Heavy Duty, she whispered, "Nineteen," and he nodded and marked the PASS box on his clipboard.

Then Heavy Duty returned to the sparring between Duke and Snake Eyes which, amazingly enough, was still in progress.

Heavy D got there just in time to see Duke do a quick, graceful move that beat all the odds and landed a solid hit on Snake Eyes, knocking him not to the ground, but back a ways, and on unsteady feet.

Among the spectators, next to Heavy Duty, Breaker looked shocked, even though it was Snake Eyes who had electricity crackling blue all over him.

Breaker whispered to Heavy D: "You ever see *Snake Eyes* take a hit? I never saw Snake Eyes take a hit. . . ."

Heavy Duty did not contradict this notion.

Then Stone was at Heavy Duty's side. "This one's a JOE," he said. He glanced at Heavy D's clipboard. "Nineteen? They're both JOEs. Live with it, Heavy D."

Begrudgingly, Heavy Duty shrugged. "Might be they're JOEs."

The facility's not surprisingly well-outfitted gym also served as a kind of lounge, with darts, billiards, chess, a big-screen TV area, and other less than strenuous activities on the periphery of all the weight-lifting, punching-bag work and serious StairMaster action.

Right now the bare-chested Duke and Rip were side by side, lifting weights. Or anyway, Duke was lifting weights. Rip was talking.

Rip nodded toward Scarlett, who was practicing her archery off to one side, and whispered, "You know what Heavy D told me?"

"What," Duke said, hefting a barbell, "did Heavy D tell you?"

"That Scarlett graduated college at *twelve*."

Duke said nothing, concentrating on the weights.

"I mean, what *is* she, anyway? Some kind of freaky genius? Who can take that, being around some kinda freaky genius? *Deadly*, freaky genius. . . ."

"I get it," Duke said, and set the barbell down. "You like her."

Heavy Duty and Breaker, his computer eyepiece exchanged for a pair of reading glasses that made him look vaguely professorial, were seated opposite each other, playing chess. They were near enough to Scarlett at the archery station to conduct a conversation with her.

She was saying, "You're going to teach *me* science? Hey, I read all the emission tomography studies when I was twelve. I'm just saying—no such thing as romantic love. It's all biology and sociology."

Breaker said, "You can't learn about love in a book, Scarlett."

Heavy Duty, his bare chest still slick with sweat from a recent workout at the punching bag, grinned at her and said, "Seems to me you'd have to kiss a guy at least *once,* before you can claim any expertise in the romance department."

Breaker thought that was very funny. So did Heavy Duty.

Or at least they did until they saw Scarlett aiming her bow at them, arrow at the ready.

Her smile was as sweet as it was nasty. "You know what's saving you, boys? Can't decide which one to shoot first. . . ."

They stopped laughing.

When she had returned to her archery practice, Heavy Duty moved a pawn and risked a further comment. "All I'm sayin' is, in my experience? When the bass gets the booty shakin' in *just* the right way . . ."

He got up and did a freaky little dance that made everybody laugh except Scarlett, who was glowering at him.

"You tell *me,* girl," Heavy D said. "Is that science? Is that biology? Sociology maybe? Or just plain *love.* . . ."

Groans of laughter followed all around, and Scarlett had to work to hide her own smile.

Rip and Duke, still at the weights, had heard and seen much of this. Anyway, Rip had.

And Rip was saying, "Ah, the hell with it. I'm *goin'* for it. . . ."

He left Duke to keep struggling with the weights, and strode off toward where Scarlett had moved onto a StairMaster.

Duke paused and called after his friend: "Rip? . . . *Rip*! Buddy, be *careful.* . . ."

Breaker moved his bishop, saying, "And into the Valley of Death rode the Six Hundred."

"If by the Six Hundred," Heavy Duty said, "you mean one damn *fool.* . . ."

Rip moved past the TV area, where Snake Eyes had taken over the space to do some fancy balancing on his two swords. The guy could walk around on the damn things, and it irked Rip a little. He swatted one of the swords out from under Snake Eyes, but the ninja took no offense, easily maintaining his balance on the remaining single sword.

Scarlett, working up a sweat on the StairMaster, was reading a book. Rip stepped up and glanced at the title, but it was in a language he couldn't read—that is, an Indecipherable Scientific dialect of English.

"That's your idea of beach reading?" he asked her.

She seemed not to notice his presence.

"Look. I guess we kinda got off on the wrong foot. I'm kind of a joker, which you may have picked up on, but I am sincere about . . . some stuff."

Her expression unchanging, she turned a page, and kept up her brisk StairMaster walk.

He got up on the adjacent StairMaster and started it going. Started walking. Kept talking: "Okay, so here's how it is: I'm attracted to you. No law against it. You're attracted to me. No law against that, either. And as for *him* . . ."

He nodded toward Snake Eyes, doing his sword-balancing act.

". . . him there should be a law against. Probably are a few. No offense, but that Zen Master, he creeps me out big time. So. Anyway. What I'm trying to say is—"

" 'We're attracted to each other,' " she said flatly, still reading.

The biggest grin in the History of Mankind blossomed. "*Thank* you!"

She flashed him a look. "That's not what *I'm* saying—it's what *you're* saying. Trying to say."

Rip walked, not getting anywhere.

"Okay," he said finally. "What are *you* saying?"

She thought for a moment. Her eyes finally rose off the pages of the book, though still did not meet his. "Attraction is an emotion. Emotions are not based in science, though certain biological reactions are sometimes incorrectly described as emotional responses."

Rip used all his willpower not to say, "Huh?"

She was saying, "And if you can't quantify, or prove, that something exists, well . . . in my mind, it simply doesn't."

Rip had followed maybe . . . none of that.

He said, "Okay, I'll get back to you on this." He stepped off the machine, and took a second to regain his balance. "Some things in life need to be . . . pondered."

Scarlett seemed about to say something, but it never got said, because General Hawk strode into the room, Cover Girl right behind him, and everyone snapped to attention.

Hawk said, "Duke, you scored in the top half-percent of all the recruits we've ever tested. Rip . . ." Something teasing came into the general's tone, faint but there. ". . . well, if we average your scores with Duke's, you pass, too."

That got a laugh out of everybody, in particular Scarlett.

The general came around and shook Duke's hand and Rip's.

"Welcome aboard G.I. JOE," the general said. "Provisionally, of course."

Heavy Duty spoke up. "It remains to be seen if you pass muster in the field, gentlemen."

Duke nodded, as if to say, "Understood."

Rip was looking at Scarlett, delighted to see that she was pleased he had passed. ·

It delighted him even more when she and Breaker yelled, "*Yo JOE!*"

And then everybody joined in and said it again. Duke and Rip, too.

CHAPTER EIGHT

Desert Storm

Dusk on the desert found the sun setting fire to the sand, turning it a brilliant orange. Unimpressed, an Arab in native dress guided his herd of camels up and down dunes in a vastness so peaceful, the idea of war might seem even more absurd than it inherently was.

And as the twilight darkened to a moon-swept night, the herdsman unknowingly crossed over a certain underground headquarters, unaware that, many feet below, security JOEs at a console were monitoring the passage of man and beast, including the use of X-ray imaging to confirm their skeletal structures.

For some time, under the full moon and glittering stars so bright the sand seemed ivory, the herdsman and the camels continued their progression, their only sounds the ones they themselves were making, the solitude of their journey soothing.

The herdsman thought he heard—or was he imagining?—some kind of mechanical *thrum*. And he had just decided that he really *was* hearing something when around him half a dozen or more mounds of sand rose in the desert floor, as if massive animals were burrowing down there, almost knocking him over.

He stared in awestruck disbelief as the mounds whipped past him and then seemed to disappear, as if submarines had been traveling just below the surface of the ocean of sand, and had decided to dive. . . .

Many miles away, down in G.I. JOE headquarters, lights were flashing on a console in the Pit's security section. A technician noted this and alerted the man next to him that sensors were detecting seismic activity to the southwest.

"Probably just a tremor," the other tech said. "But have a team check on it."

At this time of evening, the level given over to the Urban Combat Center was deserted. The JOEs on the Pit level were either involved with security, social activities, or sleep. On a rock wall beyond the eerie cement mock-city, where earlier today Duke and Rip had won their G.I. JOE status, an earthquake-like shudder was followed by the noses of what seemed to be massive drills, ten of them. And then entire cylindrical one-man vehicles with drill-bit noses emerged from the wall, bursting like toys from a piñata, to clang heavily onto the concrete flooring.

These were Mole Pod machines, courtesy of MARS Industries, though not surprisingly minus their corporate logo. The cylindrical vehicles were steel-and-Plexiglas, perhaps twelve feet in length, and resembled nothing so much as backward rockets, with the sharp blades of the drill-bit noses like petrified flames.

Ana rolled out of one, as did Zartan, Storm Shadow, and seven Neo-Vipers.

The Baroness again wore her black body armor with low-slung pistols, her brunette hair brushing her shoulders, her eyes shielded by safety glass, her face and her fingertips the only flesh showing.

Storm Shadow was in his white ninja garb, hood, swords and all, while Zartan might have been on a casual outing in his black leather jacket, black shirt, and slacks. The new breed of Viper resembled the old—black combat attire and skull-like helmets.

Ana withdrew a small gray paddle-like device that was actually a hi-tech scanner, which shot out six blue beams in a 360-degree arc. Soon, the device's screen revealed a detailed schematic of the Pit—Ana could see the layout of every room, as well as the movements of the people in them.

She pointed down a tunnel. "That way," she said quietly.

Behind her, Storm Shadow separated three Neo-Vipers from the pack and told them to guard the Mole Pods. They had made a successful entrance, but it would be nothing without an equally successful exit.

The assault force of seven moved through the cement city and its bullet-pocked facades, like ghosts floating through, haunting it—the white-clad Storm Shadow, in particular. Zartan was whistling softly, his attitude as casual as his attire.

Ana found the man's icy attitude off-putting, but this was an opinion she kept to herself. She had a job to do, and personalities needed to stay out of it. She glanced at the screen of the scanner, noting a G.I. JOE who had been creeping up on them— right now, the JOE was hiding himself behind a pillar up ahead.

She shared the screen with Storm Shadow, who, as they passed the pillar quickly, nonchalantly thrust a sword blade through the JOE, killing him instantly.

Zartan knelt over the fallen soldier, as if concerned or about to utter a quick prayer; instead, he took the man's hat and glasses. Then, as the others paused for him, he traded his leather jacket for the dead man's camouflage one.

Whistling all the way.

In his stateroom, General Hawk was in the office area, at his desk, humming a jaunty military tune.

He was going over the paperwork regarding the new JOEs, Hauser and Weems, when a crisp knock came at the door. He rose, answered it, and found his lovely blonde aide, with the smart tablet in one hand and a stylus in the other.

"Sorry to disturb you, sir."

"Not at all, Cover Girl."

"I just need you to sign here, here, and here . . ."

He did so.

Then she said, "And here, and here."

This he also did.

"Anything else?" he asked.

"No sir, just this . . ." She gave him a rare, un-guarded smile. "And another thirty-six more pages."

He grinned at her. "Maybe you should step inside."

She hugged the smart tablet to her, and began to say something, but it never got said, because the tip of a Katar dagger thrust through the tablet, having taken a path through Cover Girl's back.

As she fell to her knees, eyes large with the shock of dying, the figure of Zartan in camo-cap and jacket revealed the source of the blade.

Rushing past the dying girl, even as Hawk clawed for the pistol at his side, was the blur of white that was Storm Shadow. The general barely saw the blade, so fast was it wielded, that sank into his midsection and sat him rudely down on his office floor, his belly burning as the blood seeped out.

Hawk was almost unconscious when he saw Zartan lean over to whisper into Cover Girl's ear; the attacker was holding onto her, though she'd already fallen to her knees, and smiled as he said, "You see? I *said* I'd see you around. . . ."

Then he let her body fall to the floor, where within seconds, she was dead.

The camo-capped Zartan withdrew the dagger from the dead woman's back, sheathed it at his side, then glanced at Storm Shadow, who was regarding the fallen, unconscious general, as if wondering whether to slit the man's throat, just to make sure.

"Got some blood on your boots," Zartan told Storm Shadow. "Pity. Such nice shoes."

Storm Shadow slipped his blade into its shoulder sheath, not bothering to hide his disgust.

Zartan grinned at him. "Oh, that's right—*you* don't kill women. You're too chivalrous."

Storm Shadow paused, and his eyes in the white-hooded mask glared back.

"If *you* were a woman," he said, "I would make an exception."

Ana strode past Zartan into Hawk's office.

She leaned down and ripped the general's dog tags off his throat. Hawk's vault-like safe was nearby, and after the Baroness had swiped the dog-tag bar code on the vault's locking mechanism, Storm Shadow lifted the unconscious general up, bodily, and—using a thumb to open the man's right eye—held the man's face to the safe's scanner.

The vault clicked open.

Ana grabbed the plump, hardshell weapons case from its resting place, and the intruders left the office to the severely wounded general and his dead aide.

Storm Shadow should have slit the general's throat, because Hawk's eyes flickered open and he somehow managed to desperately roll himself over, and willed himself to lunge at a button on his desk.

A warning klaxon blared.

In the workout room/lounge, Duke, Rip, and every other JOE present leapt at the sound.

"The warheads," Duke said.

As they rushed out, Breaker paused just long enough to change the position of a chess piece on the board; but in the hall, Heavy Duty said to him, "I *saw* that. . . ."

Then hands were grabbing weapons from the rifle racks on wall mounts within the weapons locker, and JOEs—many of them in less than battle gear, interrupted in their off-duty hours, others quickly getting into camouflage fatigues at least— were hurrying, hustling into the fray.

In the cavernous Urban Combat Center, the trio of Neo-Vipers waited like weird modern statues, coming slightly to life when the voice of Ana came over their com links: *"Prepare the machines— we're on our way!"*

The three Neo-Vipers were turning to obey that order when grenades slammed into them, and tore them to pieces, doing the same to the Mole Pods they'd been guarding.

A grim-jawed Heavy Duty, in camo-fatigues, stood near a rocky wall in the UCC, a massive weapon in either hand, one of them his machine gun-cum-grenade launcher, which had just proved its considerable worth.

Ana and Storm Shadow were above, running on a gangway along the bullet-pocked mock cityscape, the heavy weapons case clutched in the woman's right hand.

Seeing Heavy Duty and the carnage he'd created, the Baroness set the case down and filled her hands quickly with the pulse pistols from her low-slung holsters, and began blasting away at the big man, who dove for cover, much of that cover promptly blown apart and knocking him to the floor, hard, his weapons skittering from his grasp.

A JOE came rattling down the catwalk and was right on them, and a sword seemed to materialize in Storm Shadow's hands. He sliced the young soldier into oblivion and sent him careening with one last cry over the railing.

The ninja paused to assess the situation. The eyes in his white hooded mask were taking everything in, including what appeared to be a pair of jet packs, their sleek golden exoskeleton-like frames mounted on freestanding vertical racks thirty feet down.

"Follow me," he told Ana.

And he leapt over the rail and dropped with cat-like grace on the floor far below.

Ana arched an eyebrow and muttered to herself, "Like *that's* going to happen. . . ."

Glancing around, she quickly formulated her own route down, clutching the handle of the weapons case in her right hand and directing a pulse blast from the pistol in her left, to blow out the far end of the gangway, causing the end of it to drop and provide her a path. She began sliding down the fallen gangway, and took out a pair of JOEs, charging in at her on the way.

Hitting the ground running, she headed for Storm Shadow, who was getting into a jet pack.

Ana yelled into her com link: *"Find the Control Room, and open the exterior hatch!"*

Then a voice filled the chamber like thunder: "Put the case *down,* Ana!"

Storm Shadow froze, and Ana turned slowly . . .

. . . and Duke was right there in front of her, with a very old-fashioned, but quite deadly, weapon in his hands: a .45.

"You heard me," he said quietly.

"I heard you," she admitted, almost pleasantly. She set the hardshell case down on the concrete floor. "Fine. Done."

Duke was mildly surprised by her compliance, and the gentle tone of her voice. That was because he did not see, coming up behind him, a Neo-Viper, getting a bead on him with a pulse rifle.

The enemy combatant had his shot lined up and was half a second away from squeezing the trigger, when a mechanical sound caught his attention, and the skull-head turned to see a forklift, loaded down with big metal plates, coming right at him.

The forklift smashed into the Neo-Viper, crushing him against a gray combat vehicle, whose own heavy armor crumpled like paper—the difference being, the vehicle could be repaired, whereas the Neo-Viper was totaled.

"Eat *that*," Rip said, from behind the wheel of the forklift.

Ana barely glanced at this, taking a step toward Duke.

"Stop, Ana," he said coldly, working to keep any tremor out of his voice. "You just *stop* right there. . . ."

But she did not, moving ever closer to him. "You can't shoot me, can you, Duke?"

And she smiled. There was nothing mocking in it, though perhaps something of the old, loving Ana.

Still, he said, "I will if I have to. If you *make* me."

"I don't think so," she said. "Deep down? You're still the same sensitive man I fell in love with."

"You fell in love with a soldier, Ana. Don't forget that . . . and don't force me, killing you."

"I know what you're thinking about," she said, and her voice was gently musical. "You're thinking about what *could* have been . . . right, Duke? You standing beside Rip, your best man. Me . . . walking down the aisle to Mendelssohn."

Best man Rip was spinning that forklift around, and charging across the bay at them. "Don't listen to her, buddy!" he called. Then to himself, as a thought creased his brow: "Was I *really* gonna be his best man?"

Duke cocked the .45 and the small sound made a

big echo. "Goddamnit, Ana . . . don't make me *do* this."

She took another step.

Duke pressed the pistol to her forehead, the snout kissing her flesh.

Nearby, Storm Shadow's cool broke as he flinched at this sight.

Catching the ninja's movement, Duke said calmly, "Move again, and I'll blow her away. This close-up, it'll mean a closed casket service."

The man and the woman were so near one another, they could feel each other's breath. The only times they'd been closer had been when they made love. Their eyes locked, in acknowledgment of that, and much more. . . .

"Do it, why don't you, Duke?" she asked. Her voice was soft, like a summer breeze. "After all . . . you already killed me, once upon a time."

Duke was strong, but he wasn't that strong; he felt himself falter, momentarily, just as another Neo-Viper came charging at him out of nowhere.

Again, Rip rode to the rescue, coming right at the skull-helmeted soldier, who fired a pulse blast at the forklift, shearing all the metal plates it was conveying, and taking the entire cockpit cage off the vehicle.

For a moment, Duke thought his friend had been decapitated. . . .

But then Rip popped up, looking stunned but very much alive, enough so to quickly recover and plow that forklight right into, and through, the chest of the Neo-Viper.

Unfortunately, the dying enemy soldier let loose an errant pulse blast, which exploded somewhere over Duke's head, and sent a shower of shattered glass and debris down on him, startling him, almost knocking him over in fact, and giving Storm Shadow the opportunity to deliver a martial arts kick that did knock him to the floor.

Ana seized the moment, and the weapons case, and went sprinting off toward the elevator platform.

Rip leapt off the mangled forklight and charged after her. But Storm Shadow lunged at Rip, slicing the man's pistol in half with one sword, metal cleaving metal, and was about to execute him with the other sword when a second ninja plunged onto the scene—*Snake Eyes!*

The dark-clad hooded ninja swung his own blade, catching Storm Shadow's with a *clang,* saving Rip's life by half an inch . . . but half an inch was enough, as far as Rip was concerned. He got out and away from the two ninjas, and fast.

Because Snake Eyes and Storm Shadow were facing off.

They lunged at each other, their blades flashing and clashing, the sound of metal on metal ringing and careening through the vast chamber, sparks flying. They exchanged an hour's worth of blows within minutes, each expert strike parried with similar skill, at seemingly impossible speed.

Finally they locked swords and, as muscle exerted itself behind steel, the two were staring into each other's eyes. Then the man in black caught the red markings on the white sleeve of his opponent, and recognized the red markings of his own ninja clan. . . .

With a cynical smile in his voice, Storm Shadow said, "Hello, brother."

Then their duel resumed, even as the remaining Neo-Vipers and more JOEs arrived on the scene, both sides immediately opening fire. With all hell breaking loose around them, Duke and Rip found themselves pinned down behind the rubble that had been the forklift and its cargo.

Elsewhere at the facility, a pair of Neo-Vipers were bursting into the Pit's Control Room, and pulse-blasting every JOE in the room into a crumpled pile of dead flesh. Then the intruders went to the controls and began to open the giant sand-dune door in the desert's floor.

With this done, the two enemy soldiers exited the Pit, leaving dead men behind, and a route of exit ahead.

Back in the Urban Combat Center, half a dozen JOEs were charging out, getting a superior position up on a gantry platform, firing machine guns at a Neo-Viper striding toward Duke and Rip. The enemy staggered from a thousand hits, allowing Duke to turn his attention toward Ana, who was fleeing toward a ramp onto the elevator platform.

He knew what he had to do, and he took aim. . . .

But the Neo-Viper had only been rocked by those bullets, not stopped by them, not with that body armor, and now fired a blast from his pulse rifle at a vehicle next to Duke, a heavy Hummer that was flung like a toy into girders that took the gantry down and sent the JOEs plummeting off their perch.

One JOE hit so hard, his weapons belt fell off, and went sliding somewhere, taking its cargo of hand grenades along for the ride.

Meanwhile, Ana had made it to the elevator platform, and had found the controls to send it up, but before it had risen far, Scarlett was suddenly there, leaping up onto the platform, her red hair streaming.

In camo-fatigues now, Scarlett deftly kicked the pulse pistol from Ana's grasp, and the two women began to fight hand-to-hand, punches alternating with martial arts moves. For a while Ana tried to hold onto the weapons case with one hand, and do battle with Scarlett, one-handed. But that was a hopeless effort, and the Baroness set the case down, and gave her full attention to her redheaded foe.

Though Ana had had no other choice, the decision was almost immediately a mistake, because in the struggle, the weapons case got kicked off the rising platform, landing on the ramp below. Locked in a violent embrace, the women—whether intending to or not—went off the still-rising platform and crashed into some crates, back at combat level.

By now, Heavy Duty had struggled onto his feet, after taking a blast that would have killed most men. A Neo-Viper, on fire but only speeded because of it, came flying out of the fiery Mole Pod area, attacking Heavy D, kamikaze style.

Not far from there, Storm Shadow had traded his sword for an elbow in Snake Eyes' face, knocking the man in black to the floor, hard, and giving Storm Shadow the opportunity to fling an explosive pellet at the cement, producing a blast of flame and smoke to cover his exit.

Elsewhere, Duke had just picked up a discarded shotgun in time to see a Neo-Viper, firing Rip's way. Duke let a blast go, right at the fumbled grenade belt, which exploded and launched the skull-headed soldier across the area and into the crashed forklift.

Rip was on top of things, following up his buddy's shotgun blast with a well-placed shot at the forklift's gas tank, which exploded into an orange-and-blue ball of flame decorated with the gray of billowing smoke, flinging the Neo-Viper into the Combat Center's generator. The enemy burst into flame and smoke, as he soaked up every volt of the ten thousand coursing through him.

That other fiery Neo-Viper, the one who'd rushed Heavy Duty, had been fended off by the big man long enough to allow the flames to finish their work. Heavy D did not have time to catch his breath before another fire-draped Neo-Viper came at him and managed something a pulse blast hadn't: decked the giant, flinging him across a stack of crates, where he hit the floor hard.

Ana was staggering up off the cartons where she'd fallen, and seeing Scarlett doing the same, she quick drew her remaining pulse pistol.

But Scarlett was wearing a camo-suit, with its near invisibility capability, and the redheaded JOE triggered the suit and seemed to melt away in front of the Baroness, who fired randomly, blowing much around her to smithereens . . . but not the invisible Scarlett.

Heavy D was getting to his feet, staggered by the fall, patting flames from his sleeves, backing away from the oncoming, flaming Neo-Viper.

Rip, seeing this, smashed glass labeled IN CASE OF EMERGENCY to free up a rocket launcher, which he held in his hands like a precious offspring; then he whirled and fired the damn thing. . . .

"Heads up, Heavy D!" Rip called.

The rocket went whipping across the entire Urban Combat Center to hit the rock arch above Heavy Duty, who dove out of the way. The arch, bearing a giant engraved G.I. JOE emblem, exploded into immediate rubble and crashed down on the flaming Neo-Viper, putting the fire, and the Viper, out.

Heavy D stuck his head up above a pile of debris and saw Rip, grinning like a damn fool, God bless him.

The big man smiled back. "Look what you did!"

"Hey, bro, you're welcome."

Elsewhere, the Baroness was trying vainly to fight an invisible opponent, unable to spot the ripples of air around her until it was too late, and she'd been struck a hard blow. One such blow sent her pulse pistol flying, and another cut a gash through an eyebrow. Ana did her best, fighting the unseen opponent, but Scarlett landed blow after blow.

Finally Ana spotted an oil pan, and flung the black liquid, spraying everything around her, including Scarlett, making her visible enough, in a black, drippy way, for Ana to leap at her adversary, and knock her to the ground. Enraged now, Ana was on top of Scarlett, choking the life out of her.

Storm Shadow was climbing into the jet pack again, which he ignited, the device powered by an arc of blue light that shot out of its engine. He had trained with similar jet packs and had no problem quickly rocketing toward the two fighting females, grabbing Ana by her arm and pulling her out of the catfight and up with him in a wide, high arc around the room, while Ana used her position to fire down with a pulse pistol at various JOEs, flinging them off catwalks to the waiting cement.

One Neo-Viper was still alive—if what those things did could be described as living—and Duke charged the S.O.B., firing blast after blast from the shotgun. He chased the bastard up the elevator ramp, and another blast of the big gun knocked the skull-face off the edge of the ramp, sending him plummeting.

With Storm Shadow and his jet pack piloting her around, however, Ana was able to swoop down and grab up the weapons case, from the base of the ramp. As a nice final touch, she swung the heavy thing at Duke, who was as far up the ramp as he could get, and caught him good with the thing and knocked him off.

He almost joined the Neo-Viper at the bottom of the deep shaft, but caught the edge of the ramp with a hand, and saved himself, though part of him died inside when he looked up and saw Ana and the weapons case flying up the elevator shaft toward the surface, courtesy of that white ninja ghost.

In the Pit's Control Room, Breaker rushed in only to skid to a stop as he saw dead JOEs flung everywhere, crushed like empty pop cans under a boot heel. He did not linger on the tragic sight, rather ran directly to a control panel and began to close the giant sand-dune door.

Storm Shadow and the Baroness were flying up toward the closing door, which they whipped through at the last possible second, sparks flying as the jet pack scraped off the edge of the swirling-shut doors, which slammed behind them as the pair flew up into the waiting embrace of a Typhoon gunship.

As the ship sped away in the moonlit, star-swept night, the camel herdsman watched it go. This, however, was not the same camel herdsman who had earlier seen strange beasts burrowing beneath the sand—that herdsman lay naked and dead on the desert's sandy surface.

The man walking in the herdsman's place, wearing his apparel, tending the camels, whistling a pleasant little tune, was another escaping invader.

Zartan.

CHAPTER NINE

Reflections

At dawn, Washington, D.C., lacked the pulse of constant activity for which the city was known, a sleepy place now, golden sunlight shimmering across the reflecting pool, the Lincoln Memorial casting a long shadow, the Washington Monument a longer one.

Within the great buildings of the nation's capitol, however, activity did indeed pulse. At 1600 Pennsylvania Avenue, for example, the current occupant of the White House was moving quickly, determinedly down a corridor, trailed by staff and Secret Service. Tall, slender, with close-cropped hair that hadn't been all-over white when he first took office, his oval face at once kind and shrewd, the president of the United States—in a well-tailored dark suit and blue tie set off nicely by his flag pin—did not break stride as he accepted a report from a staffer, skimming through as he continued on.

In a tone so even he might have been inquiring about the breakfast menu, he asked, "How many warheads?"

"Four, Mr. President," the young female staffer replied.

"Any threats? Demands?"

"None so far, sir."

A male staffer, just as young as the female, said, "We take this to mean the terrorists are unfocused, with no clear goals. Perhaps they have the black market in mind."

With a sudden stop that almost had the rest of them piling into each other, the president turned grave eyes on his people and said, "No—the lack of threats or demands can only mean one thing."

"Sir?" both young staffers said.

"It means," he said, and he began to walk again, "they intend to *use* them. . . ."

At the MARS Industries underwater base at the polar ice cap, CEO James McCullen was in the holo-chamber with projections of the Baroness and Storm Shadow—who were in a submarine speeding toward Europe—looking on. He held up an ancient iron mask, a fearsome thing that spoke of the rack, iron maidens, and red-hot branding irons.

"This was once worn by an ancestor of mine," he said. "Dating back to the 1600s, in France—they kept him prisoner in the Bastille. Caught him selling arms to both sides. The French forced him to wear it for the rest of his life—it is no doubt the origin of the Man in the Iron Mask legend. They called him Destro, destroyer of nations."

Storm Shadow's hologram asked, "Why do you

keep with you such an unpleasant reminder of your ancestor's tragic fate?"

As he looked at the mask in his hands, the mask seeming to look back at him, McCullen smiled thinly. "So that I never forget the most important rule in dealing arms."

Ana's hologram asked, "Never sell to both sides?"

"No, my dear. That is only good capitalism. The most *important* rule is to never get *caught*."

McCullen returned the mask to its museum-quality case. "Take the warheads to Paris. Have them weaponized. Then . . . I want you to test one."

Ana's eyes widened. "*Test* one?"

"Oh yes." His smile broadened. "We'll let CNN, MSNBC, and FOX News show the world just how well our new toys perform."

Storm Shadow's nod was barely perceptible. "Fear—it is the great motivator."

"Indeed."

For a moment McCullen seemed to be reflecting again, perhaps on his long-dead ancestor.

Then he said, "I have a target in mind—one the French will never forget. If we have learned anything in recent years, it's that nothing quite impresses so much as a rewritten skyline."

Ana asked, "Why the French? Why not America, or Great Britain?"

"Call me a sentimental fool, if you will. But I have never forgotten what those cowardly French-

men did to Clan McCullen. They say revenge is a
dish best served cold, and revenge taken hundreds
of years later? What could taste any colder, or
sweeter?"

In the Urban Combat Center, JOEs were cleaning up the mess, including the giant, smashed G.I.
JOE insignia. Snake Eyes was seated on a pile of
that rubble, and those cleaning things up steered
him a wide path—the dark-clad ninja had been sitting like that for hours.

Duke approached him. "Hey."

Snake Eyes raised his head and eyes looked out
from behind the mask. But he said nothing.

Duke smiled, just a little. "I know, brother.
Guess we're *all* running into ghosts, these days.
That fellow ninja of yours just looked a little *more*
like a ghost than some."

Then Duke clapped his comrade on the shoulder,
and moved on.

Snake Eyes remained as he'd been, brooding, reflecting, not on the battle they'd just waged, but on
the past, on his long-ago childhood. . . .

A drizzling rain came down as if to add insult to
injury in a Tokyo alley that was a stifling narrow
passageway between shabby fences that were lined
and littered with trash, abandoned boxes, and
scuttling rats. Above, on either side, were nests of
fire escapes, and at the mouth of the alley, half a
block down and a world away, were the gaily col-

orful lanterns, purple, yellow, blue, orange, of a brighter life lived by those who had jobs and families and goals that included more than just finding their next meal.

Here, the ten-year-old orphan boy in threadbare brown who would one day be Snake Eyes shivered in the cold rain and, desperately hungry, scavenged for food in a garbage can, like the rest of the rodents. As he moved in a grotesque buffet line from can to can, finding one scrap here and another there, he suddenly found himself washed in light.

The fence had given away to a stone wall, with a gate adorned with red clan markings, beyond which emanated a warm glow, courtesy of a temple.

He managed to climb the wall and, led by delicious food smells, found a window looking onto a kitchen, where a well-fed monk was presiding as resident chef. The room was spacious, yellow-walled, with furnishings of dark bamboo and darker wood; here and there, on the floor, and on work tables, were crates and plates of fruit and vegetables—purple cabbages, red onions, yellow pears.

Paradise, the boy thought.

When the fat monk had exited, young Snake Eyes sneaked in over the sill. He was immediately drawn to the pot of rice on a stove in the midst of the kitchen, and had lifted the lid and helped himself to a bite when another little boy, about his age, came in.

This boy had little in common with young Snake Eyes—this was a well-fed, healthy, and very likely wealthy kid in fresh white robes, sashed black.

Then the boy in white, known as Storm Shadow, yelled *"Thief!"* and plucked a meat cleaver from a small table near the stove.

That cleaver cut the air much too near young Snake Eyes for his peace of mind, and he used the rice-pot lid as a shield to parry.

What followed was a melee worthy of half a dozen adults, as the two kids used everything that wasn't battened down in that kitchen to fight each other—utensils, furniture, even precious food. The orphan kid had street skills, but the boy in white had classic martial arts training that gave him the edge.

Finally, young Storm Shadow had little Snake Eyes on the floor, on his back. And the look of triumph, as one little boy ground his foot into the neck of another little boy, would have been disturbing to just about anyone, but certainly the kid getting the foot-in-the-throat had reason to think so.

Another voice echoed through the kitchen: "Storm Shadow! *Enough!*"

A ninja master, swathed in red and orange, his eyebrows heavy and black on an otherwise hairless head, had stepped into the room.

Young Storm Shadow did not remove his foot. He said, "He was stealing, master. We need to call the magistrate."

The Master said, "Speak English, Storm Shadow.

And have you not yet learned the value of mercy? Of compassion for your fellows? Where are your manners?"

Storm Shadow removed the foot.

With a kindly smile, the Master turned to the boy on the floor, and said in English, "He is hungry. We need to invite him in, and show him the path."

Young Storm Shadow's eyes flared, and his voice was nearly shrill when he said, in English, "He's a cur! A weakling!"

"He does not fight like one."

English was something Snake Eyes did not understand, either. As he got to his feet, he wondered if had gone over a fence onto another planet.

But he understood the glare the other kid was throwing his way. And he returned it.

The grounds of the Arishikage Temple provided a paradoxically idyllic and tranquil setting for the study of martial arts—green, flowing landscape surrounded by trees, touched by colorful flowers, dotted with rock gardens, with a pond over which a wooden bridge arched. Here, students in red and blue robes trained under the watch of the Hard Master and other monks.

The two boys, paired for training, would trade blows with nunchuks, and inevitably Storm Shadow would send Snake Eyes to the earth.

And the Hard Master would look on expressionlessly.

They would duel with swords, and Snake Eyes

would find himself on his back, facing the blunted steel tip of Storm Shadow's weapon.

And the Hard Master would look on expressionlessly.

But one day, when they advanced to the smaller katana blades, Storm Shadow pressed forward only to have Snake Eyes sidestep him, and hurl the other boy to the floor. This time, it was Snake Eyes who loomed over Storm Shadow and pointed a blade right at his face.

For the first time ever, Snake Eyes had triumphed over Storm Shadow.

For once, the stony-faced Hard Master reacted, bestowing Snake Eyes a single, congratulatory clap. The small gesture was a huge insult to the other boy, however, and Storm Shadow gazed at the man who was his father, his flesh and blood, stunned that the Hard Master was happy for the other boy.

Storm Shadow slapped his katana blade into its sheath and stalked off.

Later that same day, when he was relaxing on the temple grounds, young Snake Eyes heard a loud cry—of pain, perhaps, but surprise, certainly. He ran toward the main temple building, and entered only to see the Hard Master seated on the floor before a small table, slumped there, his tea spilled . . . and his blood. . . .

A samurai sword had been plunged into the monk's back.

"Master!" the boy cried.

Looking around helplessly, Snake Eyes caught a glimpse of a fleeing Storm Shadow.

Other monks in orange and white hurried in.

One of them said, "That's Storm Shadow's sword!"

The other, pointing, said, "There's the murderer."

They could see out onto the grounds, where the boy in white was running; but the child paused for a moment, and looked back, and Snake Eyes' gaze met Storm Shadow's for one terrible moment, before the latter raced off.

Snake Eyes held the Master in his arms, and wept, begging him not to be dead; but the Master could not comply, and the nearby monks, their hands folded solemnly, could only look on in silent sadness.

As these memories flooded through his mind, Snake Eyes could have no way of knowing that Storm Shadow had been similarly occupied, sending his unblinking eyes into his own past, seated somewhere inside the Typhoon that bore him, Ana, and the warheads they'd stolen, on yet another mission of murder.

A battered and bruised Scarlett entered the barracks, checked around and, seeing that she was alone, made her way to the wall of sinks.

Looking at herself in the mirror, she peeled off her fatigue blouse to reveal the scoop-necked green

T-shirt below, so she could check the choke marks that Ana had left behind. Scarlett was tough, but her hands were trembling.

She didn't see Ripcord, stripped to his green tee as well, enter the barracks, not at first anyway, and when her eyes caught his in the mirror, she did not hide that she would prefer to be alone.

He seemed about to honor that, when he noticed the bruises on her throat, and genuine concern crossed across his features in a wave.

"Damn, girl—you okay?"

"Fine. I'm fine."

"You *are* fine in general, but specifically I'm talking about your pretty *neck,* which is not fine. Let me have a look at that."

She shot him a glare. "I *looked* at it. It's *fine.*"

Rip met her eyes in the mirror. His expression was gentle, nothing jokey or pushy about it. He said simply, "Take it easy. Just tryin' to help."

But her defenses were still up. "I know what you're trying to do."

He frowned just a little. "And what is that, exactly?"

Her mouth tightened; her chin crinkled. "I don't have *time* for this."

"You know," he said, matter of fact but with a slight edge, "not *every* guy you meet has to be a complete jerk. You *do* know that, don't you?"

His expression was touched with disappointment as he turned and started off.

She wheeled. "It's not *you*, Rip . . . it's . . . I didn't really want anyone to . . . *see* me like this."

"What, in your skivvies? We've all seen each other that way, Red."

"No. I mean, see me like *this*." And she gestured to the bruises on her throat.

"Why not?"

She shrugged and smiled sheepishly. "I don't know, exactly." The smile vanished. "I guess, it's just . . . with all the people we lost last night? Cover Girl. Maybe even General Hawk. My little injuries are just not that important."

He shook his head. "Girl, you almost died. You're *allowed* to be concerned. You can feel shook up and be no less the soldier."

He came over and turned her gently toward the mirror. "Look at you—you're still here. A lot of other good people are dead. But the bad guys couldn't kill you, and that witch Ana sure as hell *tried*. . . . You oughta let that *build* your confidence, not tear it down."

Scarlett allowed herself a glance at her reflection.

"But then, of course," Rip said, "that would be an emotional response . . . you know, one that can't be explained or quantified?"

He turned and started off.

And Scarlett watched him for a moment, before she blurted, "We're not a couple!"

He turned and looked at her, confused.

"Snake Eyes and me," she said. "We're not a

couple. We *are* close . . . brother and sister close, but . . . not a *couple.*"

Rip took that in, nodded, said, "Good to know," and walked on out of the barracks.

In the medical recovery wing of the Pit, General Hawk was hooked up to a life-support machine, unconscious.

Duke, seated nearby, was getting his shoulder bandaged up by Lifeline, their chief medical officer, a bearded fellow in his forties who was beyond unflappable.

Can you kill *her?* echoed the unconscious man's voice in Duke's mind.

Then came another mental reverberation: *Ana strangling Scarlett, squeezing the woman's throat harder, ever harder, the embodiment of pure evil.*

Lifeline, having put the finishing touches on the shoulder bandage, said to Duke, "That oughta hold you."

Duke snapped back to reality, noticing Lifeline walking away. He took in a breath, sent his eyes to the unconscious general nearby and then stood, moved even closer. He had a promise to make.

"*Graveyard* dead," he told Hawk.

In another medical chamber, at the MARS Industries secret base at the polar ice cap, the Doctor with the bizarre breathing apparatus was in hospital whites. He approached his patient, sitting up on a gurney—Zartan, for once not in black, was also in white.

"Are you ready, Mr. Zartan?"

Zartan was checking the screen of his PDA. "I was born ready, Doctor. This is going to be the achievement of a lifetime."

"Yours and mine."

"These 'Smart Robots' of yours do know what they're doing?"

"Oh yes. I programmed them personally."

Zartan's chuckle was as soft as it was nasty. "Eighteen months of studying my target, learning his mannerisms, adopting even his eating habits. . . ."

The Doctor nodded. "Losing forty percent of your muscle mass. A real sacrifice."

"That did hurt." Zartan flashed a smile. "But the devil, as they say, is in the details."

The Doctor might have been smiling; with the breathing mask, it was hard to tell. "Your commitment has been inspiring to me. I will not forget it."

McCullen entered the operating room, his manner no-nonsense. "Gentlemen—shall we get on with it?"

Zartan, still seated on the gurney, held up the PDA. "Once the ledgers are square, certainly."

"Should be there now," McCullen said, faintly irritated. "Check again."

Zartan checked the PDA while McCullen shook his head, annoyed. "It's always about the money with you, Zartan. The bigger picture eludes you."

"Money is the only way in life to really keep

score . . . *ah!* The transfer just hit my account."
The smile, ever sinister, flashed again. "Party time,
gentlemen."

Zartan set the PDA on a steel table, then he
whipped a hand out, grabbing the approaching
Smart Robot, stopping the thing. Quickly, deftly,
Zartan plucked a computer chip from under the in-
jection needle, and snapped it in two.

"I'll control my own brainpan, R2D2, thank you
very much."

Then he leaned back on the gurney and cracked
his knuckles, which along with whistling was one
of the few mannerisms that were really his own,
and said, "Let's do this thing."

The Doctor strapped Zartan down, then started
his little steel army of Smart Robots, which con-
verged on Zartan, injecting him with dozens of
long needles. He remained conscious throughout,
apparently feeling no pain.

But when a particularly long, large needle
opened an incision behind Zartan's right ear, thousands of nano-mites were fed into the patient's
skull . . .

. . . and the ever cool Zartan was cool no more—
his eyes bulging as he began to scream, as if suffering a burning pain so sharp, strong and deep, no
man had ever before experienced it.

He fought his restraints as the nano-mites began
to reshape his appearance, reforming facial bones
and changing the texture and very elasticity of his
skin . . . even changing the color of his eyes!

The Doctor beamed behind his mask, proud indeed.

McCullen, however, wore a disturbed expression.

Turning toward him, the Doctor asked, "Does my work make you uncomfortable, sir?"

"Not an issue. What's important is that I have the stomach for it."

"Do you?"

"Yes," he said, "as all great commanders must."

When McCullen had gone, the Doctor—for reasons of his own—slipped Zartan's PDA in his pocket.

"As all great commanders must," he whispered to himself.

CHAPTER TEN

Good to Go

In the green-walled medical examination room off G.I. JOE sick bay, a dead Neo-Viper was stretched out on a table like a Viking on his shield.

The sleek black body armor now had a battered look, gray from the soot and dust of battle. In camo-fatigues and T-shirts, four JOEs stood as if at the open casket at a funeral. Scarlett and Heavy Duty were on one side of their fallen foe, with Ripcord and Duke opposite.

At the moment, though, the quartet was not regarding the dead soldier, rather Scarlett and Heavy D were craning their necks to look behind them, Rip and Duke looking past the other JOEs to the back wall where Snake Eyes was gesturing to X-rays and ultrasound images displayed on a bank of flat screens.

"Nano-mites," Scarlett said. "I read about them at Oxford."

Rip said, "Well, afraid they didn't cover that at junior college."

With a gesture to the battered combatant stretched out before them, Duke said, "These guys weren't like any soldiers I've ever come up against—including the ones who *looked* like this, who attacked our convoy in Central Asia. This bunch didn't even *try* to evade fire—they just kept coming."

"And coming," Rip said.

Scarlett nodded glumly. "That's because these subjects have no control over their real thoughts—their own thinking doesn't matter. They'll do whatever they're programmed to do. Nano-mites can be programmed to accomplish different tasks in their hosts."

Rip was frowning. "Like what?"

With a shrug, she said, "Theoretically? The possibilities are endless."

"Try me."

An eyebrow lifted. "Increased speed, agility, resilience. You program, they perform."

Rip's frown deepened. "Computers with guns?"

"No. These are flesh-and-blood men, just like you, Rip. That's the genius of nanotechnology—you can make nano-mites do pretty whatever you want them to."

Duke's eyes were tight. "Mind control, you mean?"

"I don't see why not."

"What if the host body is overtaxed?"

"The host drops dead, probably." Her smile had

no mirth in it at all, and her eyes traveled from Rip to Duke and finally Heavy Duty. "But if war has taught us anything, gentlemen, it's that there are *always* more soldiers. . . . Have we seen enough?"

As they moved through the corridor, the group of five continued to talk.

Duke said, "We need to find out who's holding the leash on these dogs."

Heavy D said, "Judging by their weaponry, financing, intel, there are high-end pros. Which limits the possibilities."

Rip stopped cold, blurting, "The *weapons* case!"

Everybody else stopped, too.

Scarlett said, "What about it? We know they've got it—it's what they came for."

Rip's eyes danced. "Wonder how these snakes found a super-secret HQ so easy? It's that *McCullen* character! I bet that dude used that code he gave us, to . . . like, reactivate the tracking beacon or something."

Scarlett's eyes narrowed, and she nodded. "So McCullen uses NATO to fund his Research and Development . . . then steals back the end result."

Dark expressions passed between the five JOEs.

Duke gave Rip a little sneer of a smile. "And they say you aren't a *thinker*. . . ."

Before they'd started off again, Breaker rushed up to them, the smaller man with his trim beard and reading glasses looking ever more like an academic.

"Got her," he said, with a wolfish smile. "I have *found* her. . . ."

The group followed Breaker into the Control Room and to a big flat screen where a wedding photo was displayed—Ana and a distinguished-looking older man.

"That's her," Duke confirmed. "You found her, all right—Ana Lewis."

Breaker corrected him: "It's Ana DeCobray, now—Baroness DeCobray, if you're feeling formal about it."

"Wow," Rip said. "She really traded *up* . . ." Noticing Duke's frown, Rip added with a quick, unconvincing smile, "I mean, you know . . . in the financial sense."

Duke nodded at the screen. "Who *is* this character?"

Breaker said, "Baron DeCobray is a big-shot French scientist—born into wealth, he's supposedly devoted himself to the betterment of mankind. Runs a lab in Paris."

Scarlett's expression was thoughtful as she said, "Lab as in . . . ?"

Breaker called up an image of DeCobray standing in a cylindrical chamber front of a huge metallic framework shaft with a glowing core. The baron was in the company of a group of what were presumably fellow scientists.

"Lab as in particle accelerator," Breaker said.

Duke knew only the bare basics of what was

now on the table—the Baron's baby was an atom smasher, a device using electric fields to propel electrically charged particles to high speed, used primarily in research labs . . . like the Baron's. If there were any sinister applications, Duke wasn't aware of them.

Scarlett apparently was, however, because she said, "They're going to use the Baron to weaponize the warheads."

Duke took her word for it, and said, "Then Paris is where she's heading."

Heavy Duty shrugged and said, "So who's up for croissants?"

"I like mine," Breaker said, "with a 1945 Mouton Rothschild."

Rip asked, "How's that go with a Royale with Cheese?"

Obviously they were all on board with Scarlett's thinking, and soon they were literally onboard a Howler, cutting through the night sky at Mach three.

Now no one was making light repartee. They were silent, sitting with eyes staring straight ahead. They did not know exactly what lay before them, just that it would be hard and it would be violent. They had lost friends and comrades in the past twenty-four hours, and had defended the G.I. JOE fortress with honor and bravery, only to lose the battle. The woman known as the Baroness, aided by Storm Shadow, had won possession of the nano-warheads, and that spelled victory for the wrong side.

Duke did notice when Rip and Scarlett shared a smile, and that almost made him smile, as well. Almost. He was thinking about another mission, one in the Far East about four years ago, that did not allow for smiles. . . .

It was less than a town and more than a village, a gathering of flat-roofed buildings of either paint-peeling cement or flimsy corrugated metal, a landscape where dead cars and garbage cans seemed to be the chief decorative touch.

One road through the thick jungle got you there under normal conditions, but today—as explosions erupted seemingly randomly—a Blackhawk helicopter had been the preferred mode of travel for an insertion team headed up by Duke, and including Rip and Ana's brother, Rex, along as chief medical officer. He had his own top secret orders, the exact perimeters of which Duke didn't know.

Right now the seven-man insertion team—with Duke and Rip in the lead—were racing down a bullet-pocked alleyway. Rex, kit bag over his shoulder and a .45 Colt auto on his hip, was just behind them, crouching as he ran.

Enemy fire came their way and they returned it, moving fast, finally taking refuge behind a dead station wagon. The corrugated-metal building that was their target, the entire reason for the mission, was less than a hundred yards away. Mercenaries on guard there came around the side of the house in an assault that Duke and his men quickly took down.

Hunkered behind the car, Duke—head damp with sweat under his black stocking-cap—hand-signaled the two-man Bravo fire team to hit the front door. Machine guns at the ready, they rushed in, and no immediate sounds of hostility within followed.

Enemy fire from in and around neighboring buildings continued, as well as the jungle that choked this hellhole, and the insertion team returned fire. Duke paused to reload his machine gun, glancing at Rip beside him, who was doing the same. Rip looked a little overwhelmed.

"Double Bubble?" Duke asked his pal, offering him a piece of gum.

Rip took it and nodded his thanks.

"Always helps me," Duke said, and blew a pink bubble, popped it and grinned at Rip. "You good?"

Rip, unwrapping the bubble gum, found a weak little grin. "Yeah. . . . Anybody tell you, you a fool?"

"Everybody, all the time."

They chewed their gum and waited, even as gunfire and explosions rocked the world around them.

Finally one of the Bravo team guys was in the doorway of the shabby house. He signaled the "All clear," and Duke double-tapped Rex on the shoulder. The boyish brother of the woman Duke loved seemed small and kind of helpless, the cap making him look like a Little League ballplayer.

So Duke put steely reassurance into his voice. "You're good to go, Rex. You don't find what you're after in that lab in four minutes, get the hell out. Because that piece-of-crap house won't be *standing* in five minutes—got it?"

"You sound sure of that."

"I am—I already called in the air strike."

Rex swallowed. Nodded.

Duke gave him a smile and a pat on the back as Rex took off, running low, heading for the door. Duke's eyes never left the kid who'd been entrusted to him by both the U.S. Army and one Ana Lewis, or anyway not until the *whump* of mortars around him sent Duke's eyes to the jungle.

But Rex was safely inside now, before the mortar rounds really started to hit, and the ground near the dead station wagon was ripped apart as if by an invisible plow, and dirt and dust and God-knew-what was flying all around them.

Moving through the debris storm, Duke, Rip, and the rest of the insertion team took new cover, behind another dead vehicle.

Bullets flew at them from rooftops and windows but mostly from the surrounding jungle, and Duke and Rip would catch glimpses of the enemy, lots of them, out there in the trees and growth, firing at them, and the two soldiers would pop up and re-turn fire, as best they could.

Ducking down, Rip said, "Gotta level with you, bro!"

"I hate it when you level with me."

"Five minutes till air strike don't sound like that long."

"No it doesn't."

"Only I got a bad feeling it's gonna be feel like five *hours*. . . ."

"No argument from me on that," Duke said, and gritted his teeth and kept returning fire and reloading and returning fire.

But perhaps only a minute had passed when, in the distance, they could hear the rumbling sonic roar of jet airplanes.

Duke and Rip traded startled looks.

"No," Duke said. "No, no, no . . . too soon! It's too damn *soon*!"

But there they were, F–16s in formation, streaking across a very blue sky.

Duke's eyes went to that sad-looking, shot-up corrugated metal building.

"Rex . . ." he said.

He had promised her. He had promised Ana. . . .

Machine gun in hand, Duke ran from cover, charging toward the building, tracer fire and mortar explosions all around him. These he ignored, but the whistle of a bunker buster changed his plans, and he dove perhaps a moment before its *boom* flattened the pathetic building like a swatter does a fly.

At the same time, Duke was tossed as if God had

discarded him, and he landed hard, though the physical pain barely registered, so terrible was the emotional hurt. He staggered to his feet, a jagged bloody rip cut in the flesh, near his right eye.

Stumbling, he made his way toward the smoking, flaming rubble pile that had been a building.

When the Blackhawk came sweeping low, ready for extraction, the tracer fire and explosions picked up in intensity, and black smoke was soon washing over him. Duke stood helpless in it, as if giving in to whatever fate had next for him . . .

. . . but then Rip was there, pulling his pal from the debris, saying, "Blackhawk's waiting, bro! Come on—we got wounded!"

"I can't."

"Nothing you can do for Rex. These are our guys who *can* be helped. Come on!"

And gunfire burst all around them, as Rip pulled Duke away from the ruins of the lab house, toward the waiting chopper.

On the Howler, Rip asked Duke, "Buddy— where'd you go?"

"What? Nowhere. Just thinking."

"Isn't that what you're always warning me not to?"

"Yeah. Yeah."

"You okay? You cool?"

Duke nodded.

But as Duke stared into nothing, his expression was one Rip recognized—a certain deadness in the eyes that the survivors of combat take on, guilt mingling with resignation.

And Rip knew, should anything ever happen to Duke, he, too, would own that thousand-yard stare.

CHAPTER ELEVEN
Tour de France

On a sunny day in Paris, while tourists lazily took in the Eiffel Tower, and locals crazily maneuvered the sometimes narrow streets, a black SUV pulled up at the curb in front of a modern if unremarkable-looking facility on a side street of an industrial section.

That the vehicle was a beefed-up attack truck (known to those who used it as a Scarab) was not readily apparent, although it did possess a gray pronged prow that gave the oncoming vehicle a terrible, monstrous grin, as if the machine itself knew the terrible things planned for the city of Paris on this otherwise pleasant day.

That its passengers were unusual took only a glance as Ana in black combat attire and two skull-helmeted Neo-Vipers exited; so did Storm Shadow, although the ninja had traded his usual traditional attire for a dapper vested white business suit, and seemed the most normal, unless you noticed the killer-coldness of his eyes. The trio headed into the building with dispatch.

They crossed the nondescript lobby so fast that the two security guards behind the desk had only time enough to look up and see their fate flying toward them—throwing stars, courtesy of Storm Shadow, that sank deep into two untroubled, un-furrowed foreheads.

The Neo-Vipers got behind the desk, threw the slumped, dead guards to the floor, and took up a defensive position.

Baron DeCobray, in a white lab coat, was seated at a control station in the circular chamber whose colossal size was nonetheless barely able to contain the massive particle accelerator. Still, lab techni-cians found space enough to swarm around the atom smasher, taking readings, making adjust-ments, all under the watchful eyes of the Baron, who also had a wealth of flat-screen monitors to keep track of.

So perhaps he could be forgiven for not immedi-ately noticing the intruders who'd entered into his domain, not until Ana was at his side. She had al-ready given the bulky nano-mite weapons case to Storm Shadow, silently instructing the natty ninja to hang back.

Which he did, ready to take on any opposition, in the unlikely event any of these science techies got ambitious.

The distinguished scientist looked at his wife and could only find one thing to say: her name. "Ana . . . ?" His eyes were huge with not only her unexpected, out-of-place presence, but the bizarre black apparel into which her slenderly shapely form had somehow been fit.

"I need you to do something for me, darling," she said. "And I don't have the time to explain or to argue."

He looked past her at the ninja in the stylish white suit, hovering in the background, with the hardshell case in hand, the startled eyes of the techs all around the chamber glued to him.

The Baron asked, "Who *is* this creature?"

She answered by beckoning Storm Shadow to join them. He did, setting down the weapons case at DeCobray's workstation. Then the ninja snapped open the lid and revealed the four nanotech warheads in their cushioned berths.

For all his brilliance, all DeCobray could do was gape at the softball-size warheads in abject shock.

"Time is wasting, dear," Ana told him.

"I don't understand," he managed. "What *are* these things? What in God's name is going on here?"

"They're warheads, dear," she said with a lovely smile offset by cold dead eyes. "And I need you to weaponize them for me."

That stopped him for a moment. "And . . . if I refuse?"

Her shrug was barely perceptible. "Then we'll kill *everyone* in here. You last, of course."

Then, as if the comment had been for the ninja and not the husband (and perhaps it had been), Storm Shadow pulled a nine-millimeter automatic—

a conventional one, not a pulse pistol—and shot, seemingly at random, one of the technicians.

This threw the chamber into chaos—cries of outrage and fear, and an almost comic collision of the workers as they did their best to get as far away as possible from the menacing white figure with the gun.

DeCobray shouted in French, "*Do not panic! Stay at your posts! I will handle this. . . .*"

This seemed to calm the techs somewhat, though DeCobray himself had an expression of utter terror as he faced his wife and her killer crony.

The Baron said, with strained dignity, "This is a civilian laboratory. We do not have the correct programming protocols for weaponizing those . . . things."

She gestured to the open weapons case. "The protocols are in here."

But he did nothing.

"I told you, darling," she said tightly. "I don't have much time. And neither do your *associates,* if you don't get on with it."

Through nearby city streets, another sleek but otherwise unremarkable-looking vehicle, a silver maintenance van, was out-maneuvering even the Parisian taxi drivers, fabled as the most skilled and reckless on the planet.

Heavy Duty, at the wheel, called out to his fellow JOEs in the rear of the van: "Time to suit up, boys and girls!"

Breaker was in the rider's seat, at a high-tech

terminal—as usual, he was strictly support on the mission, though he was in combat attire, too.

In back, Snake Eyes was loading his guns while Scarlett was helping Duke and Ripcord get into the bulky, metallic-silver accelerator suits, for which their training had been brief at best.

More than ever, the effect seemed to Duke a futuristic football uniform, right down to the helmet (albeit with full-face clear visor with heads-up-display) and shoulder pads.

By now Duke was mostly into the thing, while Rip was needing the bulk of the help—or pretending to, since that help was, after all, coming from Scarlett.

Unwrapping a little pink rectangle of bubble gum, Duke noticed Breaker catching him in the rearview mirror. On Breaker's grin, Duke broke off half the gum for him, passed it forward, and popped the rest in his own mouth.

Breaker said, "Hope you can multitask."

"Yeah?"

"Fight and chew bubble gum at the same time."

"Not fighting yet."

"You will be."

In the laboratory, a tremendous whine echoed through the chamber as the particle accelerator came to life, humming an even tone, its rod starting to glow yellow.

Storm Shadow backed up a little, which earned a little glance from Ana. He shrugged, as if to say,

What? She was glad to see he still had at least some human reactions left in him, besides rage. . . .

The pale, nervous technicians were somehow doing their jobs, quickly finishing up what was needed and then backing away from the accelerator.

In French, the Baron said, *"Commence primary ignition."*

And then he hit a switch.

The particle accelerator charged, and began hurling atoms through mile upon mile of underground tunnels. Within the accelerator, in a glass vacuum chamber, the four warheads began to spin. Then, as the power grew, they began to rise, as if elevated by a supernatural power and not the will of science, still spinning, hovering now as they did.

The Baroness and Storm Shadow watched with cool curiosity as the noise inside the chamber began to build. The atoms—catapulting faster and faster through the tunnels—bombarded the warheads again and again.

Finally, came a loud *boom*!

And the warheads slowly sank back down, their spinning ceased.

DeCobray pressed another button and, with a mechanical click, the glass vacuum chamber extended from the accelerator. Technicians opened the chamber and, most carefully, removed the green-glowing warheads, carrying them in gloved hands as if conveying to cribs sleeping babies prone to noisy waking.

When the warheads had been slowly replaced in their case, Storm Shadow shut the lid and worked the latches till the plump oversized briefcase was shut tight; then he took it in his right hand, like a worker hefting his lunch box on his way to the factory.

"Careful," DeCobray told the ninja. "They're *alive*."

Storm Shadow said nothing.

"Thank you, Leon," his wife said to him.

He just looked at her. "So this is the face of evil . . . the oh so beautiful face of evil. . . ."

These words seemed to rattle her, if ever so slightly, as if something in his words or perhaps his tone had pierced a hard veneer that extended well past her battle armor.

She could sense Storm Shadow watching, and this sent her protective walls back up.

Then she approached the Baron and kissed him—seemingly, a passionate kiss, and the likes of which their marriage had not before seen. He seemed unable to help himself—evil or not, this was his wife, this was the woman he loved, and his lips were still on hers when he gasped, his eyes popping, as the blade entered his back.

The Baron DeCobray slumped to the floor with the handle of the shorter but no less deadly katana blade sticking out of his back.

"I told you," Storm Shadow said to Ana. "I *said* if he touched you again, I would kill him."

"I heard you," she said, a lilt in her voice as they headed out, "the first time."

As the Baroness spoke these coolly cruel words, the silver van was racing toward the lab, so close Heavy Duty and Breaker could see the building out the front windows.

"All right now," Heavy D said, "stick to the plan. Snake Eyes and Scarlett, you take the front way in. Duke, Rip . . . you two around back. Breaker here is our eyes and ears—he'll stay in touch via helmet communicators, and you do the same as necessary. I call the shots from this seat— you do *what* I say, *when* I say. Any questions?"

There were none, not even from Rip.

Breaker said, "Almost there—better get your camo-suit on, Scarlett."

But before Scarlett could even begin to put on the invisibility suit, Ana and Storm Shadow emerged swiftly from the facility's front doors and climbed into the back of their black van, followed by a pair of skull-domed soldiers who got in front.

For a split second, both sides could see into the other's vehicle—including Duke and Ana, whose eyes locked and made that fraction of a moment seem an eternity.

Snake Eyes and Storm Shadow shared a similar prolonged split second.

"Okay," Duke said, "what's Plan B?"

But Snake Eyes was already moving past Duke, to lunge out the van's side door, just as the black van whipped past.

Rip was still struggling with his accelerator suit, with its various latches and buckles. "Get that, willya, girl? Get that latch!"

"I'm *getting* the latch," she snapped.

Duke clicked one last suit buckle and leapt out after the van, which in its quick getaway careened and slammed into a bus—hurting the bus worse than the Scarab.

Within the van, Ana was saying, "Don't worry, boys—we're insured."

On foot behind them, Snake Eyes was getting wide-eyed, curious looks from the normally ultra-blasé French citizens—perhaps they didn't see a black-clad ninja running down the street every day. He sprinted past a young hand-holding couple onto a footbridge just as the black van had taken the turn under it, slowing some to do so.

This allowed Snake Eyes to launch himself off the footbridge, and land square on top of the enemy vehicle. Within, Ana and Storm Shadow glanced up, having heard the *whump* of that landing.

On top of the Scarab, the air rushing by, Snake Eyes held onto the vehicle's roof rack with one hand, and with the other touched a button on his wrist communicator. A small yellow light began a steady flashing.

And back in the silver van, still pulled up in front of the lab, a tracker beacon appeared on Breaker's rider's seat monitor.

"Planting a tracking signal," he said into his mic,

"is well and good. But don't let go of that truck, Snake Eyes. Hang on and take the ride."

Finally, Rip clicked the last latch on the accelerator suit, and was ready to get into the thick of things. He thought he and Duke looked like a couple of robots, out of a Japanese cartoon. But cool. Cool.

Heavy Duty, behind the wheel, caught Rip's eyes in the rearview. "You be careful, bro—those suits are worth millions . . . each."

"Millions," Rip said. "Got it."

Promptly, Rip exited the side door of the vehicle, into the street, and fell on his tail on the pavement.

"This baby is tricky," he muttered, picking himself up to send a salute to the stunned-looking Heavy Duty, through the windshield.

"Won't happen again," Rip said into his helmet mic.

And a passing car slammed into him with a *whack*!

In the silver van, Heavy Duty winced.

Fifteen feet away, well-protected by the suit and more embarrassed than hurt, Rip picked himself up again.

"Sorry!" he yelled at the car that hadn't even stopped to see if he was all right. "Well, pardon me, and excuse *moi* heinie!"

Then he got his bearings, saw where Duke was in the street super-running up ahead of him, and took off after his pal, leaping like a gazelle. Or anyway, a wounded gazelle. . . .

Back in the silver van, Heavy Duty was saying, "Well, Scarlett? Are you in or out of this fight? I say, we gotta get in."

Scarlett seemed to be mulling that, but really she was watching a motorcycle messenger who was pulling up just outside the Baron's lab, unaware of the carnage within. She pushed the van side door open and was right there when the young male messenger hopped off.

"Excuse moi, monsieur," she said to him, affably conversational.

He replied in French—roughly: *"Hello, cutie— what can I do for you?"*

Eyes narrowing, she said, also in French, *"You can give me your bike."*

And she jumped on the thing, and sped off.

The messenger goggled at the beautiful redhead, disappearing down the street on his motorbike, but seemed to have nothing to say. In any language.

Elsewhere, the black Scarab was ignoring traffic, going in and around cars, and up on the sidewalk when necessary, earning much swearing in French from terrible, indignant drivers on a busy thoroughfare.

On top of the van, Snake Eyes was still taking the ride (as Breaker had instructed), if barely clinging to the top. He began to fire his pistol into the roof, an activity Ana and Storm Shadow below duly noted with less than extreme distress: the bullets slamming into the metal only created dents.

"Tenacious isn't he?" Ana said, about as concerned as Bugs Bunny with Elmer Fudd on his tail. She had the weapons case open beside her, in back of the van, and was prepping a warhead.

The other vehicle was maintaining an incredible speed, considering the traffic, but now the Neo-Viper behind the wheel took measures to go even faster. He hit a button and, from the grid, extended the Scarab's prongs, which lost their toothlike appearance to become a sort of shovel that could—and did—slide rudely in and under the car up ahead, lifting and tossing the vehicle out of its way, like a snowplow clearing a path. The sounds of metal meeting metal combined with honking horns and shrill French swearing in a kind of symphony of destruction.

Duke and Rip, running in the street at accelerated speed, glanced at each other in a *did-you-see-that* way.

Then Duke said, "Here we go—take it up a notch!"

Up ahead the Scarab was dispensing with more cars, using that metal extension to hurl other vehicles out of the way, leaving crunching metal and screeching tires and even burning cars in its wake.

As the two G.I. JOEs ran ever faster, a chunk of metal dropped off Rip's suit, and he flashed a concerned look at his sprinting partner, saying into his helmet communicator, "I think something just fell offa me—is that bad?"

Breaker's voice from the communicator said, "Uh, no . . . *you'll be fine.*"

The "you'll be fine" part was reassuring; but Rip wasn't crazy about the "Uh, no . . ." bit.

Up a ways, Snake Eyes was struggling to maintain purchase and stay aboard the speeding Scarab. One of the cars flipped by that shovel-like thing hurtled up over the black van right toward Snake Eyes, who leapt onto the flying car, running across it as it spun over the Scarab, like a bizarre log-rolling event.

But when he landed, Snake Eyes was right back home again on top of the black van, his feet firm.

As cars catapulted around them, crashing and sometimes exploding, Duke and Rip—aided by their accelerator suits—leapt over and around the ruined vehicles. Not far behind them, Scarlett on her commandeered motorcycle came around a corner into this melee, sweeping past drivers and passengers stumbling bloodily out of crashed cars.

And then a Peugeot flew over her, narrowly missing her head.

"My God," she said, "it's raining cars!"

From the communicator, Breaker said, *"It's raining* what?"

She didn't bother to respond, too busy watching vehicles flip and fall all around her (and around Duke and Rip).

"Guys!" she yelled. "Use your Gatlings!"

Rip didn't need to be told twice—he let rip a salvo of slugs at the Scarab using the forearm-mounted machine gun. Bullets bounced off its hull, ricocheting all around, including Snake Eyes up top of the vehicle.

He glared back at the approaching Duke and Rip, as if to say, *Hey! I'm* working *here!*

Rip, on the run, shrugged, as if to say, *I didn't* hit *you, did I?*

On her motorbike, Scarlett zoomed up behind Duke and Rip, and yelled, "That armor's too strong! Switch to *missiles*!"

Heavy Duty had long since left his spot at the curb in front of the lab, driving madly now as Breaker in the rider's seat struggled to keep track of the signal moving swiftly about on his monitor.

"Go left!" Breaker said. "They just turned onto the Champs-Elysées!"

"Great," Heavy D muttered. "The frickin' *scenic* route. . . ."

The Scarab was speeding toward the Arc de Triomphe, plunging through the roundabout traffic as if no one's safety was any concern, including their own. But the black van was not invulnerable: When an SUV T-boned into its side, the Scarab was knocked into the flow of slower traffic.

That jarred Snake Eyes off his perch—though he managed to cling to the roof rack with one hand, his body dangled by a window just long enough for Storm Shadow to see him, and lock eyes with his brother ninja.

Then Snake Eyes pulled himself back up onto the bullet-dented roof.

Duke and Rip were only seconds behind when a

passing truck trailer got in their path, and Duke skidded under it while Rip darted around the thing. They, too, wound up caught in the flow of traffic around the monument that was the Arc de Triomphe.

Rip said, "Last time I ever follow your tail into a mess like this."

"You're following *my* tail?" Duke asked, astounded. "I thought I was following you!"

Zooming up on her motorbike, Scarlett spotted the black van as it raced around the monument; she gunned the bike's engine, taking it and her right through traffic, slaloming around cars and trucks, jumping the bike up over the curb to leap over a chain-link fence. Then she cut through the Arc de Triomphe, dodging stunned and scared tourists.

Now the chain-link fence was in her way again, on the other side, this time. Swiftly, she drew her crossbow and fired a bolt, cutting the fence. The chain dropped as she raced by, and she came up right behind the black van as it blasted away from the roundabout, onto another street.

Duke and Rip were perhaps a second behind her.

Many streets behind, but hauling butt, Heavy D in the Brawler was saying to Breaker, "They're driving right into the heaviest traffic in Paris! What the hell kind of escape route is *that*?"

Suddenly Heavy D thought he knew the answer to his own question; and the way Breaker was looking at him indicated the communications expert was thinking the same damn thing.

"Widen that map out," Heavy D said.

Breaker, nodding, said, "I'll plot a route. . . ."

He did.

Then Breaker said, tentatively, "Maybe they're not trying to escape . . . maybe they're heading somewhere."

Heavy D knew, but he asked anyway: "A possible target?"

"Yeah. Someplace with a lot of . . ."

The screen gave Breaker the position of the Scarab, and also the position of what lay just ahead of it. He felt a thin icicle of fear melt its way down his spine to leave behind a shiver.

Together, the two men said, ". . . metal."

They could see it, even from blocks away, the potential target: *the Eiffel Tower.*

The black van was smashing through any vehicle in its path, leaving a trail of twisted-metal destruction laced with licking flames and billowing smoke for Scarlett to dodge on her borrowed bike, and for Duke and Rip to leap over, testing the limits of their accelerator suits.

From their helmet communicators came Breaker's voice: "Guys—you have *got* to stop them!"

"Yeah," Scarlett said offhandedly, "we're working on that."

"I mean *right* now—they're going to detonate one of the warheads on the Eiffel Tower."

In fact, the tower was looming up fast in front of Duke and Rip.

"Oh, man," Rip said. "That's just *mean.* . . ."

Snake Eyes, still atop the Scarab, heard Breaker as well, and he, too, could see the Eiffel Tower growing ever larger before him. He drew his katana sword and plunged it through one of the dents he'd made shooting the car roof, and the blade went through, a sword in a magician's box, almost spearing the Neo-Viper driving. He repeated this process several times, narrowly missing both the passenger-side skull-head and Storm Shadow.

Inside the van, Ana spat a command: "*Finish him!*"

The driver heaved the wheel and slammed the side of the Scarab into a semitruck, knocking Snake Eyes off the other side.

Scarlett, not far behind, saw this and yelled, "*Snake!*"

But Snake Eyes managed to hit the pavement just right, and spider-scurry under the van, where he clung desperately to its undercarriage.

Within the vehicle, Ana yelled, "He's *under* us now! He's underneath. . . ."

The Neo-Viper on the rider's side swung open the door and leaned out, aiming a pulse pistol under the Scarab at the ninja clinging stubbornly to the car's under belly.

But Scarlett quick-drew her crossbow again, and shot a bolt at the Neo-Viper's pistol, knocking it out of his hand as it went off.

The skull-helmet turned toward Scarlett and she fired again, catching him in the eye slit and sending him tumbling out onto the pavement in her path. She nimbly dodged his tumbling corpse.

Ana, watching this from a window in the van, said, "That redhead is starting to piss me *off*."

At this, the Baroness quick-drew a pulse pistol and leaned out her window to take a shot at Scarlett, blasting the bike's front tire away, causing the bike to pop up high, and Scarlett herself to go flying like a discarded rag doll. She was dropping fast toward the unforgiving pavement . . .

. . . when, a split second before she would have hit, Rip reached out and caught her, like an eloping bride dropping from a second-story window into her waiting groom-to-be's loving arms.

Rip skidded to a stop, and set her down as gently as he could manage under these conditions, just as Duke raced past.

Scarlett's lovely face was inches away from his sweaty one. He could see that she was genuinely impressed, and in the midst of all this chaos and cruelty, he had one hell of a happy moment.

"Nice save, Slick," she said.

"C'mon, girl—don't go bein' *nice* to me. I'll get all confused."

He shot her his best grin and took off after Duke.

The silver van with Heavy Duty at the wheel screeched up next to her.

Breaker leaned out the passenger side window and asked, "Need a ride, pretty lady?"

"I've heard smoother lines," she said, but got in.

Meanwhile, Rip was catching up to Duke.

"Where you been, Rip?"

"Stopped to get a latte."

Up in the Scarab, Ana could see the two men coming at her, still coming, and quickly she keyed a console.

Side panels slid open on the outer vehicle, revealing racks of missiles. A target scanner locked onto the accelerator suits, and soon two missiles were streaking back toward Duke and Rip.

"*Dive!*" Duke yelled.

"*Whoa!*" Rip yelled back.

With no time to get out of the way, they dove and rolled in opposite directions, extreme kinetic energy hurling them forward. The two missiles *whooshed* between them, and hit various unlucky parked cars, exploding them to scrap.

That was when Rip's suit began to spark and buzz and pop and spark some more.

Into his helmet communicator, Rip said, "Now it's *sparkin'*! Is *that* bad?"

"*Yeah,*" Breaker's voice admitted. "*That's bad.*"

"Good," Duke said, not in response to Rip and Breaker, but at seeing he had a straight shot at the black van, which he took, shooting off a wrist-mounted mini-missile.

The missile slammed into the back of the vehicle, low, shaking it.

Within, Ana almost dropped the glowing green warhead she was prepping.

Storm Shadow gave her a look, then said, "Tell

me—is there *any* man you've met who doesn't want to kill you?"

"That's generally one of the two things they want," she said, and keyed another button, opening a rooftop panel in the Scarab, revealing a pulse cannon.

The nasty-looking cannon swiveled and fired back at Duke and Rip, knocking them both down, the high-tech suits the only thing keeping them alive as they whammed into walls and cars.

Rip's suit began to spark and buzz and pop again, and started powering down. . . .

Then the black van tore away around a corner as Duke and Rip were just starting to slowly pick themselves up, to the confusion of the shaken locals staring at them from sidewalks, windows, and doorways.

Into his helmet communicator, Duke said, "Damnit! We've *lost* them."

CHAPTER TWELVE

In the back of the silver van, Scarlett—a headset on—had the French officials on the line. Breaker, up front in the passenger seat, noted a change on the central of his several monitors—the two blips representing Duke and Ripcord had gone suddenly stationary.

"Priorité urgente code trois," Scarlett was saying, *"huit, sept, un. Attaque terroriste immediate sur la pour d'Eiffel."*

Breaker said to driver Heavy Duty, "Sensors indicate a pulse blast. They're *down* . . ." Into his headset he said, "Duke? Rip! Are you guys okay?"

Duke's voice came from dashboard speakers: *"Damnit, we* lost *them!"*

Breaker had the black van on his monitor, showing it rounding a corner. "Cut through that building across the street!"

Duke swiveled and saw what seemed to him the ass-end of a structure, and said, "There's no damn door!"

Heavy D's voice came over Duke's helmet com: *"Make one!"*

Duke did as he was told, charging right at that building, smashing through a brick wall beneath a sign advertising a Chinese laundry.

Rip followed, lagging a little, running at normal speed now, thumping his suit like it was an appliance on the fritz.

"Breaker," Rip said, "my suit's not *right*! Not working!"

"Blast must have knocked it offline," came Breaker's voice. *"Give it a few seconds to reboot. . . ."*

"I don't *have* a few—"

But that was when Rip thumped his chest a good one, and suddenly the thing powered up, catching him off-guard and flinging him haphazardly through the hole in the wall that Duke had made.

Duke was already through the building, after surprising some Asians doing laundry and catching the attention of some attractive young women shopping in the lingerie store as he went speeding through, exploding out a wall onto the street and revealing what was going on in one of the shop's dressing rooms, much to the chagrin of various clients trying items on.

Halfway out into the street, Duke came to an abrupt stop and leveled his wrist-mounted rockets at . . .

. . . nothing.

Puzzled, he looked around at not much, since

pedestrians and drivers around here had pretty much run for cover by now.

"Where *are* they?" he asked his communicator. "I don't have any of them in view."

Breaker said: *"They're on your six!"*

Duke spun and caught the speeding hood of the black van, which smashed into him but, thanks to the accelerator suit, did no real harm. He pushed back at the vehicle, gloved hands on the hood, and dug his boots into the road while the vehicle's motor gunned, trying to run him over or at least push him out of the way.

But Duke's heels were dug in, and he was slowing the Scarab down, with chunks of pavement flying from the grooves his boots were making as it backed him up.

Finally Rip burst through the building, plucking and discarding a stray lace brassiere from his helmet, and looking around urgently.

"Duke?" Rip asked, eyebrows up, seeing the Scarab pushing Duke, and Duke pushing back. . . .

Rip took off after the vehicle (and his pal). The van was charging toward a busy intersection, threatening to crush Duke in the criss-crossing traffic—and Rip figured that suit could only do so much.

Duke threw himself up onto the hood of the van just as an SUV crashed into it. Then he tumbled up over the roof and crashed to the concrete, and was getting to his feet just as Rip caught up.

"Come on Duke!" Rip said. "Stop screwin' around!"

"I'm fine," Duke said. "Thanks for asking."

Then they ran after the Scarab, the two men neck and neck now that Rip's suit was working again.

Within the silver G.I. JOE van, Scarlett was leaning up to watch Breaker's monitors, one of which showed the black Scarab speeding through streets on an obvious course toward the Eiffel Tower.

"They're evacuating," Scarlett said, reporting what she'd just heard in her headset.

Breaker said, "We're only two kilometers away."

Heavy Duty said into his wrist com, "Snake, man! We are out of damn *time*. . . ."

Still clinging like a barnacle to the undercarriage of the black van, Snake Eyes removed one hand to free up his pistol. Then he started shooting out the tires, figuring *that* would stop the bastards . . .

. . . but the tires refilled—and *resealed*—themselves, after every shot!

Snake Eyes, seeing what was up ahead, let go, slipping back between the right and left sets of wheels, and tumbling away from the speeding vehicle.

Within the Scarab, the occupants saw Snake Eyes falling away.

"He gave up!" Ana said. *"Finally!"*

"No," Storm Shadow said. "He *never* gives up. . . ."

They turned their heads back to the front windshield, which revealed a guard arm down at a railroad crossing, a Metro Train seconds away.

The black van smashed through the guard arm onto the train tracks, but not in time: The Metro slammed into the vehicle, launching it, sending it airborne hood-over-tailpipe.

Rounding the corner, the speeding silver van had its turn to see the railroad crossing up ahead, the Metro Train flashing by, and Heavy Duty, Scarlett, and Breaker could only wonder if they had time to stop. . . .

Duke and Rip saw the train, too; but they were running so fast, even trying to stop wasn't an option.

Duke said, "Oh, hell!" and propelled himself into the air, his boots barely scraping the top of the train while his friend plunged headlong through an open window, right into the passing train.

"Coming through!" Rip called, as he flew across an aisle, past stunned commuters, smashing out the far window in a shower of safety glass.

The black van had crashed hard to the cobblestone street and was still tumbling, sparks and flame and flying metal everywhere, taking out other vehicles like bumper cars. One stalwart citizen had been opening the door to his parked car, which was gone now, though he still held the disembodied door.

Nearby, Rip was bouncing across several parked cars, like a pinball racking up a great score. Then, finally, he came to an ungraceful halt on the roof of a parked car, while Duke crash-landed on the sidewalk next to his friend.

The silver van had managed to screech to a stop before colliding with the passing train, on the other side of which Duke and Rip were on their feet now, lifting their visors to share stunned, battered expressions.

Duke asked, "What happened to you?"

"I cut through the train, man. Where the hell did *you* go?"

Duke lifted a finger skyward. "I jumped *over* the thing."

Rip's eyes grew large. "You mean, we can *do* that stuff?"

"Sure—didn't you read the manual?"

"There was a manual?"

Rip was giving his friend a *now-you-tell-me* look when the black van, or what was left of it, skidded between them, coming to a shuddering stop up ahead a ways.

Ana and Storm Shadow, beaten and bloodied, crawled out, the weapons case in Ana's left hand, a machine gun in her right. The Neo-Viper who'd been driving was dead, half-crushed, looking like a beetle who'd met the wrong boot-heel.

The Baroness glanced at the corpse contemptuously. "Next time, *I'll* drive. . . ."

A small crowd was gathering on the sidewalk nearby, typically low-slung Parisian buildings watching mutely from either side of the cobblestone street.

A woman, looking chic in a business suit, approached Ana and asked, in French, *"Oh my God—are you all right?"*

The bloody, battered Ana gave her a look, and showed her the machine gun. "Are you *kidding* me, honey?"

Back at the silver van, the others G.I. JOEs were still caught at the train crossing.

Scarlett yelled into her headset: "Duke? Rip? Have you *got* them? We're cut off by the train!"

Duke had made it to the remains of the Scarab and climbed up on top of its crushed roof and got a view of Ana kneeling in the street, the weapons case open—while Storm Shadow was loading a launcher with a warhead, its plump, tapering tip glowing green with the nano-mites payload.

Ana grabbed the kill switch, then slammed the case shut as Storm Shadow ran fast as hell toward the looming landmark tower. Then the woman in black followed, keeping pace.

Duke said into his helmet-com: "Damn—they've armed a warhead."

Then he and Rip took off after them, just as the remains of the black van exploded, blossoming smoke and flame for them to run through.

In a towering glass-and-steel office building nearby, a red-vested, bow-tied, mustached milquetoast of a delivery man had just entered a spacious foyer filled with sunlight from a glass-lattice roof many floors above.

He was looking down through his thick eyeglasses, checking an address on his clipboard while at the same time doing his best to contain a bundle of colorful "Bon Voyage" helium-filled balloons; to his frustration, one of the balloons slipped his grasp and floated up to the lattice-glass ceiling.

What else could go wrong today? he wondered.

He was shaking his head with the unfairness of his lot in life when Storm Shadow burst in through the doors just behind him, bumped him roughly, and the rest of the balloons floated up to join their mate.

Storm Shadow made for a spiral staircase, and he wasn't there yet when Ana entered, giving the delivery man another jarring jostle. She had the weapons case in one hand, submachine in the other, the small device that was the nano-mites "kill switch" attached to her belt now.

As Storm Shadow was lunging onto the spiral staircase, Ana instead leapt a low wall and propelled herself right into a glassed-in elevator, already filled with businessmen and—women.

She set the hardshell case down and brought the bulky weapon up.

Huge eyes were on her as she said, "Get . . . out. . . ."

The elevator emptied like mice fleeing a particularly nasty cat.

"Nice shoes," Ana told the last woman to exit.

The woman did not say thank you.

As Ana's elevator rose, she could see down into the spacious lobby where Duke and Ripcord were rushing in; and they spotted her, too . . . *and* Storm Shadow, making his way up that winding staircase.

"You get the missile launcher with the warhead," Duke told Rip, "and I'll go after the kill switch and the weapons case."

"Typical," Rip said with a sour smirk. "*You* get the girl, *I* get the bad guy. . . ."

Then Rip was speeding up the spiral staircase, in full view of Ana in the glass elevator; the deadly woman then turned her attention to Duke in his accelerator suit as he leapt up onto support beams and started to climb.

Ana leveled her machine gun at the climbing Duke and let loose a volley, blowing out the glass on that side of the elevator, bullets peppering glass walls behind Duke even as he leapt from beam to beam, dodging her shots.

Below, working folk were on the run, yelling, screaming, under a dangerous rain of glass debris.

By this time, Ana was out of ammo and had switched to her pulse pistol. Aiming through the skeletal frame of the now largely glass-less elevator, she unleashed a powerful shot that blew out an entire wall of glass, launching Duke into, and through, a conference room.

Elsewhere in the office building, Storm Shadow bolted down a corridor, the missile launcher in his hands. Terrified office workers scurried and even dove out of his path. He stopped and kicked down a door, but wasn't pleased by what he saw in the room beyond.

When he kicked down the neighboring door, however, he found himself bathed in sunlight, and was very pleased. . . .

Lifting the missile launcher to his shoulder, he lined up his target—the Eiffel Tower, picture-postcard visible out a nice big window, just a few blocks away.

Rip, seconds behind Storm Shadow in that same corridor, came to a skidding stop, seeing Storm Shadow with launcher poised and a clear line of sight.

"Don't *do* it!" Rip blurted.

Storm Shadow flicked off the weapon's safety, his finger settling in on the trigger.

Rip dove at the ninja, linebacker-style, just as the missile launched, the warhead smashing out the window while Rip's tackle took Storm Shadow through a wall.

Duke burst through a staircase door to find himself on the roof seeing Ana as she raced across its glass lattice-work. Both were moving fast, but momentarily froze when they saw the warhead zooming away from the building, headed straight for the famous tower.

Down in the silver van, itself racing for the same destination, Heavy Duty, Scarlett, and Breaker saw the missile streaking past.

"*Mon Dieu,*" Breaker breathed.

"We're too late," Heavy Duty said.

Scarlett said nothing, though her horrified expression spoke volumes.

The impact on the side of the tower created an earth-shattering roar. The silvery nano-mites clung to the metal structure and began to feast like the hungry mechanical bugs that they were, some of the tiny things bouncing off the tower and falling toward the ground, a shimmering wave of them soon engulfing a street lamp and still more covering a passing ice-cream truck like a dripping silver coat of paint.

Breaker said, "They'll spread through the entire city like the plague. . . ."

Heavy Duty said, "They're going to eat this town. *Alive.*"

Scarlett, into her headset, said, "Duke—you have *got* to get to that *kill* switch!"

On the glass roof, Duke and Ana were separated like gunfighters on a dusty western street, waiting for the other to draw. He had to get that kill switch on her hip. He gave her a tight, determined look, but she only smiled.

Quickly, he took off after her across the roof.

Meanwhile, Rip found himself—courtesy of several walls he'd burst through, battling Storm Shadow—in the office building's kitchen, with a pissed-off French chef cursing and fumbling for a knife or cleaver to fend off these intruders.

"Yo, Mr. GQ," Rip said to Storm Shadow, who was staggering to his feet. "I am gonna seriously have to kick your tail now. . . ."

But as Rip charged forward, Storm Shadow snatched a pot of bubbling Bearnaise sauce from a burner on the stove, and flung the hot stuff right at Rip, most of it splattering across his visor, momentarily blinding him. Reaching for a sword, Storm Shadow was ready to finish his foe, but was distracted by the sight of Snake Eyes charging down the hall toward them.

Chatter in Storm Shadow's earpiece preceded the ninja making a hasty exit, leaping through a glass window in a shattering shower.

"Come back here!" Rip yelled, wiping the sauce from his visor. "Did I say I was *done* with you?"

But Storm Shadow was busy plummeting amidst glass shards for several floors, only to catch himself on the edge of the Typhoon gunship that was picking him up. . . .

Snake Eyes was in the kitchen now, helping Rip to his feet. Wiping the sauce off hadn't really worked, so now Rip was lifting his visor—just in time to see Storm Shadow outside, rising up with the Typhoon.

"Look at that coward run from me," Rip told Snake Eyes.

Had Snake Eyes been prone to speech, he might have told Rip just how close he'd come to dying.

On that glass-lattice rooftop, Duke was chasing Ana across the expanse even as the Eiffel Tower began to tremble unsteadily in the background.

When Ana reached the edge of the building, expecting her ride to be there, the Typhoon was late.

She spun, blasted with the pulse pistol in Duke's general direction, ripping the rooftop like a sheet of paper, only these were sheets of glass, and Duke was hit by a wave of shards and chunks and slivers and chips and slabs.

Then Ana's Typhoon arrived, and as if stepping from one room to another, she left the building and entered through the gunship's side hatchway.

But Duke had fallen under the impact, the suit protecting him from cuts and worse, the glass floor under him a memory. He caught himself, barely, on a steel lattice.

Then he leapt up and leapfrogged quickly over the lattice, from beam to beam; and when he reached the building's edge, he summoned all he and the suit had left, and leapt, thirty feet across empty air.

Rip saw this from the window of the mostly demolished kitchen, his buddy leaping toward the open hatchway of the hovering gunship.

"Duke! You damn *fool* . . . !"

Duke tumbled into the enemy craft, and found himself right next to Ana and Storm Shadow—the kill switch no longer on the woman's hip, but in her hands now.

And Duke snatched the device into his own grasp, and hit the TERMINATE button before his host and hostess even had the time to react.

The nano-mites flashed like a dying firefly's last gasp, and dropped harmlessly to the ground. In their wake, an entire section of the tower's base was gone, and the famous structure began to creak and groan . . . and tilt, giving the Leaning Tower of Pisa a run for its money.

But everywhere the nano-mites had spread, they stopped, falling lifelessly, harmlessly to the earth or the floor or the pavement.

In the silver van, a smiling Scarlett said, "Way to go, Duke."

Heavy Duty said, "Not bad. Not bad for a damn rookie."

But within the Typhoon, Ana was smiling bitterly at her guest. "Congratulations, Duke—you just saved Paris. Most of it, anyway."

Storm Shadow had no congratulations to deliver— instead he tasered Duke and dropped him to the hard floor of the gunship.

And as the Typhoon flew past and vanished into the sun, the Eiffel Tower lost its valiant battle with gravity and structural integrity and, before becoming just so much scrap metal, made a magnificent crash and splash as it dropped into the Seine.

CHAPTER THIRTEEN
Going Rogue

On the cobblestone streets, ambulances were rushing with sirens going, police cars doing the same, when they weren't pulled over, cordoning off intersections. Sidewalks, whether given over to tourists or business folk, were clogged with frightened pedestrians whose faces were streaked with dust and tears.

Near the crashed black van, the JOEs had gathered, with only Snake Eyes among the missing. Right now, Heavy Duty—in dark T-shirt and trousers—was yanking one of the dead skull-helmeted soldiers from the wreckage. Breaker, in his hi-tech surveillance suit, was clearly not a tourist or a local, neither of whom would likely bend over a dead Neo-Viper and yank off the corpse's helmet.

Scarlett, however—in brown leather jacket and jeans—might have been a tourist or a local, but as she moved into position to help Breaker out with the body, she too seemed anything but an Everywoman.

As they did this gruesome work, Rip came running up and quickly peeled off his helmet and removed the bulky gray pieces that made up the accelerator suit. His T-shirt and trousers beneath were soaked with sweat, and overall he had the look of a nearly drowned pup.

Scarlett looked up to ask him gently, "You okay?"

He swallowed thickly. "Bastards got Duke."

Heavy Duty nodded. "We know."

Rip's eyes were tight. "What are we gonna do about it?"

"Get him back."

"How?"

"That we *don't* know. Just yet. . . ."

Breaker had gotten a needlelike port plug from somewhere on his hi-tech suit.

Rip asked, "What you are up to?"

"I am about to plug in," Breaker said, kneeling over the skull-headed subject, "our friend here's cerebral cortex."

"That right?" Rip nodded toward the corpse. "In case you haven't noticed, the dude is dead. Hate to break it to you, but him and his cerebral cortex? They ain't gonna tell you much. . . ."

But far away, under arctic ice in the MARS Industries underwater base, the company CEO clearly disagreed with Rip's assessment. James McCullen was watching Breaker at work via a button camera mounted inconspicuously on the dead Neo-Viper's helmet.

Urgently, McCullen turned to the Doctor, who was at his right arm. "Destroy that unit immediately."

Without even a nod, the Doctor withdrew his PDA from a pocket of his dapper gray suit and tapped a key, summoning this particular Neo-Viper's file. Then he clicked a button labeled "Terminate."

And back in Paris, the JOEs gathered around the enemy soldier's corpse saw it snap rigid, and begin to shake.

Rearing back, Rip said, "Dude's still *alive!*"

Scarlett, shocked (as were they all), said, "He *can't* be! He's got a two-inch needle in his head!"

Rip gestured to the quivering body. "You ever see a *dead* guy rock 'n' roll like that before?"

Then the Neo-Viper topped his first feat by beginning to decay before their eyes, the heavy battle armor remaining but the human within seeming to rot.

And soon they could tell why: *Thousands of nano-mites were doing their silvery, slithery thing, literally eating away at flesh, revealing bone, then eating that, too.*

Scarlett, frowning, said, "There must be some kind of remote self-destruct his masters triggered. . . . Breaker, you gotta *hurry.* . . ."

Breaker continued swiftly to scan a blinding series of images stored in the dead man's brain, even as the nano-mites continued consuming the Neo-Viper—his legs, his chest, his arms. Memory flashes froze on an image of Ana boarding the Typhoon on a snowy airstrip, with a backdrop of snow-covered mountains.

And then the nano-mites reached the head of the dead soldier, and consumed that, as well.

Breaker yelled, "No! *Damn* it!"

Back in the underwater MARS HQ, McCullen watched a monitor that gave him Breaker's frantic face, silently yelling at the disappearing Neo-Viper; and then Breaker, like the dead man, was gone, replaced on the screen with the words: UNIT 308 TERMINATED.

McCullen sighed in relief, then flashed the masked doctor a smile.

"They got nothing," he said.

The Doctor did not reply.

In Paris, on the cobblestone street, Breaker continued to stare, crestfallen, at the now empty Neo-Viper suit in his arms.

A stunned, devastated Rip knelt next to Breaker. "We're screwed. *Duke* is screwed. . . ."

"Maybe not," Breaker said, and smiled just a little.

"What do you mean?"

Breaker put a hand on Rip's shoulder. "Relax—I got everything it was possible to get."

"Then . . ." Rip frowned in confusion. "What was the '*No*' and the '*damn it*' for?"

"For McCullen," Breaker said. He tapped the button-cam on the helmet, which rested on the pavement with the rest of the now empty battle suit. "The bad guys were watching us."

They got to their feet, Rip saying, "So what did you get?"

"Admittedly, not a great deal—just images."

"You told me to relax! C'mon, man—you're supposed to be good at this junk!"

"I am the *best* at 'this junk,' " Breaker said tightly. "Nobody else could do what I just did!"

If tempers were frayed, they were about to get torn, because around them weapons were raised by a group of French police and soldiers, the former appearing to be the Parisian version of SWAT, the latter battle-ready paratroopers . . . all having an outing at the JOEs' expense.

Their leader said, in French, *"Put your hands in the air!"*

Scarlett immediately did so.

So did everybody else—except for Rip, who was scowling.

"Wait, what're you doing?" he said to his comrades. "We're the *good* guys! Tell these bozos we're the good guys!"

Scarlett shook her head. "Hands up, Rip."

"Man, we don't have time for this," Rip insisted, getting pissed off. "Duke *needs* us!"

"Standing orders," she said coolly. "No engagement with friendly forces. Hands up, Rip."

Rip wasn't having any. "The only friendly force *I* give a damn about is Duke."

And he racked his sidearm, raised it to fire in the air, but he clicked on an empty chamber.

Then the French forces rushed him, knocked him down, night-sticked him and generally roughed him up as the other JOEs were cuffed.

Scarlett yelled, *"Rip!"*

Rip's last thought, before he passed out from the pain, was, *Man, the girl* does *care. . . .*

And unseen, crouching on a fire escape on a nearby building, Snake Eyes was watching, watching it all.

In Washington, D.C., in the White House's Oval Office, the president was pacing behind his desk.

The young male staffer was saying, "We're still trying to locate the three remaining warheads, sir."

The president asked, "What's the status of the G.I. JOE unit?"

"They've been detained by the French government. They're being held in a military prison."

The young female staffer said, "As you can imagine, the French are, well, fairly upset."

"Of course, they're upset! Chaos in the streets of their national capital—would we be pleased?" He paused, and then his tone was cool: "Get me the French ambassador."

The holding cell was a Plexiglas box with a few metal tables in it, in the center of what appeared to be an otherwise empty prison cell block. French soldiers, heavily armed, were positioned all around the chamber, as if the four men and one woman within were all potential Hannibal Lectors.

On a TV monitor outside the Plexiglas cell, CNN was airing amateur camcorder footage of the Eiffel Tower making its big splash into the Seine. The network had already aired other amateur video of Ripcord scuffling with French cops and troops.

At a table beyond their clear cage, they could see a French detective curiously poking around Breaker's surveillance suit, which they'd made him strip out of, and pieces of Ripcord's accelerator suit.

Breaker rushed to the nearest Plexiglas wall and pressed his hands against its coolness; baseball-size holes were drilled here and there, to provide air for the caged animals.

"Please, monsieur!" Breaker called out in French. *"Please don't touch that. It's very dangerous, and expensive, and ..."*

But the detective was paying no need.

"Okay," Breaker breathed, and threw his hands in the air. "He's touching it."

Heavy Duty, on his feet, glanced at Rip, seated at a table and holding an ice pack to the back of his head, where he'd taken a bad blow courtesy of a French SWAT guy.

Disgustedly, Heavy D said, "Nice going, Slick."

Rip glowered at the bigger man. "Did you say something?"

Scarlett stepped between them. "It's not Rip's fault. He's just . . . emotional about his friend."

Heavy D arched an eyebrow. "Emotions, Scarlett? You're goin' *there*?"

She did not reply, rather went over to Rip and, indicating his head wound, said, "Let me have a look."

"I'm fine," Rip said, a little testy. "I'm cool."

She shrugged, and gave him a smile. "Just trying to help."

He nodded thanks, but stayed behind his wall.

Somewhere out there, a door opened noisily, and everyone craned to look.

Suddenly all their moods brightened, even Rip's: General Hawk, in a wheelchair but otherwise looking fit and very much himself, in beret and full United States Army uniform, was rolled in by Snake Eyes.

Right up to the Plexiglas wall.

"General!" Scarlett blurted.

Had that wall not been there, she'd have run up and hugged the man . . . at least, until she remembered her place.

General Hawk pushed up with his arms and got to his feet, giving a dismissive glance to the wheelchair, which Snake Eyes dutifully rolled out of the way. He seemed perhaps a shade unsteady on his feet, but General Hawk was back from the dead, which brought relief and even happiness to his Alpha Team at an otherwise very dark moment.

With no preamble, the general—whose expression was grave and showed no sign of enjoying this reunion—said, "The French have agreed to release you under my supervision . . . on one condition."

They waited for it.

"None of you may ever return to the City of Lights . . . ever."

Heavy D shrugged. "Could be worse."

The general went on: "It *is* worse. G.I. JOE has been declared a 'rogue unit' . . . characterized by the French and American governments as 'uncontrollable.' "

The caged JOEs exchanged startled, unhappy expressions.

Hawk went on: "All of you have been recalled by your respective heads of state. You're to report back to the Pit, for a final debriefing. As of twelve-hundred hours, Paris time, today . . . G.I. JOE has been shut down."

None of the G.I. JOE team said a word—they were too shaken to do so.

And General Hawk was clearly the most devastated of them all.

By dusk, the Typhoon was rocketing through orange skies and smashing through the sound barrier with an ear-tingling sonic boom.

Within the warship, Storm Shadow—his natty white suit with a bloodstain here and a split seam there—sat in a meditative state. Duke was seated across the way, his robot-like accelerator suit off, a soldier now in T-shirt and trousers and bindings, and he struggled against the latter.

Ana, on her feet, glanced at Duke, then—making sure Storm Shadow was too preoccupied to notice—walked back down the fuselage toward the man she had once agreed to marry.

"Save your strength," she advised, not entirely unfriendly. "You're going to need it."

He just looked at her. "Why haven't you killed me?"

She shrugged. "Actually, McCullen has something special in mind for you."

He didn't bother asking what it was. "What *happened* to you, Ana?"

Her eyes flashed. "*Now* you care?"

Duke had been hit with a lot today, but those words hit him harder than a pulse-pistol blast.

"I'm . . . I'm sorry," he said. "I truly am. I'm sorry about Rex, Ana. Sorry I couldn't bring him home."

"Save it, Duke. I don't do forgiveness. Fresh out of amnesty, too."

She began to walk away.

He strained forward, not just at the bindings. "Ana, this isn't *you*—this isn't the woman I fell in love with."

She turned, and—for just a moment—her face softened. "*You* abandoned *me*. Or, anyway . . . the woman I used to be. *That's* who you let down."

As he stared at her, he felt his insides getting ripped apart in a way that hurt far worse than any bullet or chunk of shrapnel could manage.

Four years ago, on a dreary wet afternoon, at Arlington National Cemetery near Washington, D.C., mourners were dispersing.

Soon Ana—folded American flag in her grasp, her raincoat a somber black—stood there alone but for a lone soldier shielding her with an umbrella, no family, and not Duke, either, as she stared at her brother's memorial.

Not enough of Rex's body had survived to even justify a body bag, and this grave was as empty as Duke felt, watching from his Indian motorcycle in a lane fifty yards or so away. He had let her down.

They shared a common grief, felt an agony obvious in both their faces; but they could never again share anything else.

Without approaching her, he drove away and out of her life, figuring it was the kindest thing he could do for her, and hoping he was not just being a coward.

In Paris, after General Hawk had secured their release, Breaker was the first out of the Plexiglas cage. He paused at the table where his surveillance suit lay, and reclaimed it, got into it.

As they exited the holding cell, Rip said to Heavy Duty, "What about Duke? G.I. JOE shut down, that's a damn shame, but are we just gonna forget about him?"

The big man's face was so impassive, it might have been carved from stone. "We have our orders."

"That right? What if it was one of you? What if the men from MARS had Breaker right now, or Scarlett? What would you do, then?"

"Everybody!"

It was Breaker.

He waved them over to view a small monitor on his surveillance suit, where they could see images of the Neo-Viper's memory flashing like a fast-forward on a DVD player.

Then, at Breaker's bidding, an image froze . . .

. . . on McCullen himself, standing with a group of Neo-Vipers as they prepared to board that gunship on a snowy airstrip.

Scarlett leaned in. "Looks pretty remote. Might be a good location for a base."

"What else are they doing there?" Breaker asked, but frustration was in his voice. "So we've got snow. That narrows it down to what, a third of the earth? . . . Wait, what's that? His shadow?"

Breaker zoomed in on the image and tapped the wrist-mount keyboard, calling up a blur of mathematical calculations.

Rip asked, "You got something?"

Scarlett was ahead of everybody but Breaker. She said, "Spherical trigonometry."

Rip said, "Must've missed the day they covered that."

Scarlett continued: "If you know the height of an object, the length of its shadow, and time and date, you can figure out its location."

"Definitely didn't cover this in Shop Class," Rip said.

Breaker said, "McCullen is one-hundred-eight-three centimeters. His shadow is forty-two centimeters. Image has decayed three point six percent . . . which means it's fifty-one hours and seventeen minutes old."

On the monitor, the spherical triangles were replaced by a set of coordinates that blinked steadily at the assembled eyes.

"Polar ice cap," Scarlett said.

"There's your snow," Rip said. "Man, you guys are smart. Maybe even smarter than me."

They turned to look at Hawk, who with Snake Eyes had come quietly up behind them.

Heavy D asked, "What do you say, sir?"

"I told you people to report to the Pit," he said. "But, uh . . . I don't recall specifying exactly when, or what route to take."

Scarlett smiled just a little. "Maybe a northern one?"

The general allowed himself his own rumpled smile. "I suppose there's no point being a rogue unit if you don't *really* go rogue, every now and then."

Snake Eyes and Heavy Duty fell back, as

Breaker's suit projected a 3-D holograph of the globe, a series of spherical triangles flashing across the six continents.

"Would a 'Yo JOEs?' be appropriate," Rip asked, "about now?"

It was.

CHAPTER FOURTEEN

Strike Fear

The MARS Industries gunship zeroed down through the night over a stretch of ice near the opening of a huge cavern, guided by runway lights glowing under the ice.

After the Typhoon made its smooth landing, Storm Shadow and Ana, in a fur coat, exited the craft with Duke, wrapped up in a dark coat so generously provided him by his captors. The prisoner was escorted out by a pair of Neo-Vipers, who seemed to need no winter attire, their black battle armor doing just fine to keep out the cold.

As the group headed into the cave, the Typhoon rocketed away, disappearing back into the blackness.

Within the cavern, Duke counted only two more of the skull-helmeted soldiers on guard, and noted a futuristic-looking jet fighter plane, which he later would come to know as a Night Raven.

Storm Shadow clicked a handheld remote, and a hidden wall that seemed to be ice but obviously wasn't, slid away to reveal a hi-tech diving bell awaiting them.

Duke, who had been behaving himself, seized the moment to grab the weapons case from Ana's grasp, and haul for the outside, although the danger of the awaiting, freezing vista might make escape a Pyrrhic victory.

Storm Shadow spun toward the fleeing prisoner, throwing stars in hand, while the Neo-Vipers raised their pulse rifles.

But Ana stepped forward and raised a hand. "No! McCullen has plans for him. Don't *kill* him!"

Nonetheless, Storm Shadow hurled a star that went whistling across the cave, nailing Duke in the shoulder, sending him down hard on the icy floor, still holding onto the case, fumbling with it, then staggering to his feet, ripping the star from his shoulder and jamming several of its sharp points into the eye slit of a charging skull-headed guard.

The Neo-Viper dropped on his back, apparently dead; but others were on Duke now, beating him mercilessly.

Ana jogged up, calling, *"Enough!"*

Storm Shadow retrieved the weapons case, glancing at the bloodied Duke with contempt. "And what was your plan? Run three thousand miles across the ice? You'd have been dead in minutes."

The ninja in the now rather shabby white suit shook his head and walked off, muttering, "Stupid damn soldier. . . ."

Duke's eyes went to Ana, daring to thank her for saving his life.

She returned his gaze, but he couldn't read anything there, not even hatred.

Which was a start.

In the Control Room of the Pit, General Hawk—already free of the wheelchair—came charging into the technician-filled chamber. His face traveled from JOE to JOE at their stations.

"As you know," the general said, "we've been shut down, and kicked out. You're all under direct orders to return to your respective national bases. . . ."

Looks of disappointment were exchanged all around the big room.

"But," Hawk said, his eyes narrowed, his head tilted, "I have something I need to do, which is not covered by our standing orders. You might even say it violates those orders."

Everyone seemed to perk up.

"If any of you leave now," he said, "I certainly won't hold it against you."

It was the Alamo moment—the point where the commander of the doomed mission had drawn a line in the dirt and told everyone willing to stay to step over it. According to legend, all but one of the beleaguered warriors at that forlorn Mexican mission had crossed over to stay and fight and die.

There was no line in the dirt to cross, but the JOEs were all standing a little taller, looking a little stronger, and staying right at their posts.

General Hawk smiled. "All right. I've already had your individual orders sent to your stations—you'll see immediately what's needed of you." The smile vanished, the eyes went steely. "Now, let's get to work."

And the Control Room burst into a flurry of activity.

Already, a sleek next-generation atomic submarine emblazoned with the GI JOE insignia was cruising through night waters.

In its conn tower, washed in the sub's greenish lighting, Rip, Scarlett, Snake Eyes, Heavy Duty, and Breaker were going over a three-dimensional map of the polar ice cap.

"Man," Heavy D said, "even a society girl don't have that much ice."

Breaker shook his head. "It will be like trying to find a needle in a coal mine."

Rip gave the guy a look—no question, Breaker spoke English well, second language or not; but sometimes the guy got things a little twisted up.

"That's needle in a haystack, bro," Rip said to him.

"Oh," Breaker said. "Right. Dully noted." A small light began flashing on his ball-eyepiece. "Now that's strange. . . ."

Rip asked, "What are you duly notin' *now*?"

Scarlett asked, "What is it, Breaker?"

Breaker had a half smile going. "When they stole the weapons case, I set my scanner for the tracker beacon . . . just in case it came back on . . . and guess what? It has *just come back on.*"

Rip shook his head and grinned. "That's my boy, Duke. That's my boy."

At the polar ice cap, the diving bell was operating as a kind of elevator for the party that had recently exited a Typhoon gunship. The bell came shooting down out of a shaft, rocketing toward the underwater facility.

When the diving bell entry port opened, two more Neo-Vipers were waiting, on guard duty; but also James McCullen himself stood there, patiently waiting, in a sharply tailored black suit with matching black shirt and even a black tie, its silk adorned, as usual, with an oversize tie tack of the family crest.

The CEO's eyes first moved to the hardshell weapons case in Storm Shadow's grasp. Noticing this, Storm Shadow stepped up to McCullen and immediately opened the case, showing him the three remaining warheads with their green-glowing cores.

Like a man stroking a beloved child's head, McCullen ran his fingers over the deadly objects, then nodded for Storm Shadow to close the case back up.

"Take them to the drones," he instructed. "I want them ready to launch in one hour."

With a curt nod, the ninja said, "It will be done."

McCullen turned to Ana with a smile that nauseated Duke. "My beautiful Lady of the Lake," Mc-Cullen said to her. "My condolences on the recent death of your husband."

"Thank you."

Then he kissed her.

And she kissed him back, though her eyes were on Duke.

Which was not lost on the seemingly impassive prisoner, but he still could not read her—was she punishing him, or . . . something else?

Duke's host turned his creepy smile on his new guest. "Isn't it funny," he said, "with the entire balance of power in the world about to shift, how two boys can still have a stare-down over who gets the girl?"

"Hilarious," Duke said, stony-faced. "Would you like to see something else that's funny as hell?"

McCullen raised an eyebrow and leaned closer.

Duke head-butted him.

Instantly, the Neo-Vipers were on Duke, pummeling him to the floor.

McCullen, amused or trying to appear to be, was wiping a small trickle of blood from his nose. "Very droll, Captain Hauser. You do have a sense of humor." He gestured to the Neo-Vipers to stop.

They did.

McCullen looked down at the bloody, battered warrior. "The interesting thing about my men here is that they still think the same thoughts they always did . . . they just can't act on them anymore."

Duke said nothing. He was too busy bleeding.

"Instead," McCullen was saying, "they do exactly what I want them to do . . . and I imagine that must be very frustrating."

Then the MARS CEO got right in Duke's face and said, "Just so you know—I intend to make you very unhappy."

"You've got a head start," Duke said. "I already am."

McCullen straightened, glanced at Ana, who had been watching this display with what seemed to Duke to be conflicted eyes.

Then the CEO beckoned the Neo-Vipers to help Duke up, and make the prisoner follow along behind him.

McCullen's domain was a world of indirect blue-hued lighting and hard gray metallic surfaces, nuts and bolts unhidden in an openly industrial manner as cold as the man who ruled here.

As they walked down a rounded corridor, the little group passed a window onto the deep ocean, where a school of fish was swimming by. The group of humans had gone on and so did not notice one fish breaking away from the school.

Even so, they would have had to look closely to tell that this was not a fish at all, but a mini-robotic underwater spying system.

In the conn tower of the G.I. JOE sub, Breaker was saying, "Picture's coming online now."

The team was gathered around Breaker, who

was watching what the "fish" was seeing, courtesy of a monitor.

Brow tensing, Scarlett said, "It's a *perfect* location—nearly undetectable, easily defensible. . . ."

Rip, leaning in, said, "Duke has gotta be in there somewhere."

"Duke and those warheads," Heavy Duty put in.

Breaker sighed, sat back. "We *have* to find a way inside—a *quiet* way. . . ."

Snake Eyes gestured to the diving bell cables, which had just come up on the monitor.

"Elevator cables," Scarlett said. "That means they've got a surface entrance."

Right now, though, Breaker was zooming in on a massive weapon.

Rip reared back. "Whoa—what the hell is *that* baby?"

"Would appear to be," Breaker said thought-fully, "an automated, phased array turbo-pulse battery."

"Try it in English."

"A really big gun."

Heavy Duty went over to the sub's commander, told him to take them up, and then Heavy D led the team down the sub's central corridor.

"I'll lead the main assault from outside," he told them, "and keep 'em busy. You four infiltrate the facility from above. You know the mission: find Duke . . ."

". . . grab the warheads," Rip said.

"And kill all the bad guys," Scarlett said.

"Roger that," Heavy D said.

Snake Eyes, of course, said nothing.

But they all knew when it came to killing bad guys, he was the man.

In a corridor of the deco-metallic underwater base, Duke was trailing behind McCullen and Ana, flanked by Neo-Vipers with pulse rifles ready.

Duke asked, "So what else do you have in mind for the warheads? You've taken down one of the most beloved wonders of the world. What next?"

McCullen flashed a smile back at his prisoner. "You've taken to your G.I. JOE training well—that's good. Here you are in a hopeless situation, and you're still trying to develop intel. Never say die, I suppose."

"Then you won't mind answering my question."

His hand gesture was casual. "I don't mind. Isn't it obvious? I'm a businessman—the latest in a long line of arms dealers. I'm going to use the warheads in a most profitable way."

Frowning, Duke said, "McCullen, millions of people are going to die, if you launch those warheads. What is it you *want*?"

The CEO stopped and turned to Duke, making him stop. "Why, Captain, I mean to strike fear into the hearts of every man, woman, and child on this planet. Then they will turn to the individual who wields the most power."

Duke sneered at him. *"You?"*

"Oh, no. Not me." McCullen seemed genuinely

amused now. "Don't strain yourself over this, Captain—you're not seeing the whole picture."

"Then paint me the whole picture."

McCullen's smile was the kind seen in small boys who enjoyed tearing the wings off flies. "I wouldn't want to spoil the surprise."

In the Control Room of the Pit, a technician was turning toward General Hawk.

"Teams have been deployed, sir," he said.

"Good," Hawk said. "Now give me a satellite uplink. I want to see everything that's going on, in real time."

"Yes, sir."

And the tech made that happen.

In the MARS underwater HQ, McCullen and Ana were leading Duke and his two skull-helmeted escorts into the bustling flight control room, alive with technicians hunkered in at various stations, several of the seemingly countless monitors displaying three large aerial drones waiting in vertical launch bays.

Duke took in the drone missiles on those monitors and could not keep the horror from registering on his face—*he knew what McCullen was about to do!*

Ana's eyes met his briefly, and then she turned away. Duke could only wonder if he had seen a hint of remorse in her eyes. . . .

Then he felt the eyes of someone else on him,

and Duke turned to see a bizarre-looking figure, a slender man in a tailored suit but with unhinged-looking hair, a blue monocle and an otherworldly gizmo, a breathing device of some kind, that hid his lower face and even covered his nose in metal tubing and hard black rubber.

"Meet the evil genius behind all of this," Mc-Cullen said lightly, gesturing to the well-dressed monster. "This is the visionary we call the Doctor. . . ."

"My genius," the Doctor said modestly, "lies only in taking what others created to the next logical step. All modern gains in science are, after all, made through theft."

Duke had nothing to say to that. But what he most of all didn't understand was why this oddball was looking at Duke as if *he* were the apparition.

McCullen said, "You'll have to excuse the Doctor's humility. When I found him, he was a mere—"

"Who is this?" the Doctor said, cutting off the CEO. "Another 'recruit'?"

"Yes," McCullen said. "A rather unwilling one, but . . . yes."

"I'll prepare him for the procedure," the Doctor said, and began to exit, directing the Neo-Vipers to bring Duke along.

Duke and Ana exchanged one final look, and neither noticed McCullen's eyes on Ana as she watched Duke go.

Before long, Duke, in bare chest and surgical trousers, was strapped onto an operating table. A

Neo-Viper guarded the door, and squat Smart Robots were warming up, at the bidding of the Doctor, behind his main console. These midget robots,
Duke figured, were the madman's scalpels. . . .

"The atomic bomb that was dropped on Hi-
roshima," the Doctor was saying, "destroyed seventy percent of that city—seventy percent. Did you
know that, Duke?"

The casual use of his name by this fiend made
Duke give the Doctor a closer look.

Under all the horror-show accoutrements, was
there something familiar about this creature?

Wind blew steadily across a remote stretch of
arctic ice that looked as though it might have ex-
isted just like this for centuries.

But a moment later, that ice began to crack like an
eggshell, then to rupture and finally erupt as the conn
tower of the G.I. JOE submarine came crashing
through. When the sub had ground to a halt, a forward hatch opened and two Rock Slides launched
out—heavily armed vehicles on skis, compact crafts
that looked like sleek metallic bugs, with blue-and-
white camo-coloration, appropriate to the surroundings. They landed hard on the ice and went speeding
away.

Soon, near the entrance of the ice cave that
served as access to the underwater MARS Industries HQ, two Neo-Vipers were standing guard,
one of them noticing, way off in the distance, a
slight glint.

Then an arrow bolt jolted the skull-helmeted soldier, and threw him ten feet back through the cave entry, while the other Neo-Viper turned and dashed to throw the alarm.

But he, too, was hit by a powerful arrow bolt, sending him for a ride that did not stop till he fell dead next to the other skull-headed corpse.

The two vehicles raced up and into the cave, then skidded to a stop next to the dead soldiers. Two Rock Slide doors slid open, and Ripcord and Scarlett got out of one vehicle, Breaker and Snake Eyes out the other. They were in protective winter gear, as white as the snow around them, with fur-rimmed hoods and protective amber-toned goggles. Towering nearby was the next-generation jet, which got a whistle out of Rip.

"Our boy McCullen," he said, "sure has got himself some toys."

Breaker gestured toward the wall of apparent ice. Snake Eyes, using his katana, sliced a circle in that wall, yanked it out, and through the newly created aperture, the diving bell cables yawned before them.

No diving bell, though.

Breaker said, "Maybe we should slide down."

Snake Eyes shook his head, clearly doubtful about that suggestion.

Scarlett agreed with that silent assessment: "The water's too cold—even with survival suits, our hearts would freeze."

Rip gave her a smile. "Not mine," he said.

She almost returned the smile, but that was when the entire ice cave began to shake and tremble.

The JOEs exchanged alarmed looks, then ran as one outside, where a large circle of ice near them had begun to melt.

And then the first of McCullen's drones burst through the water where ice had been, exploding up before their eyes and launching into the washed-out blue of the arctic morning sky, peeling away to the east.

Before they could react, a second missile exploded up like a terrible flower, and peeled off to the west.

Then they heard the third one about to rocket up and Snake Eyes, thinking fast, sprinted into the cave, jumped in one of the Rock Slides, and zoomed back outside. On the skis-mounted vehicle, the ninja hit a weapons switch, prepping two heat-seeking rockets on either side of the sleek bug.

When the third drone launched upward, two hundred yards away, Snake Eyes locked onto its exhaust and fired.

The heat-seekers raced up after the drone and knocked the thing out of the sky, exploding it into metal fragments, fiery shrapnel dropping far down into the waiting arms of snow and ice.

In the spacious flight control room of the underwater base below, technicians noted the explosion on several of their many monitors.

One tech elected himself to deliver the bad news to McCullen: "Sir . . . we lost one."

McCullen, Ana, and Storm Shadow were looking up at the monitor screens.

"Lost one?" McCullen said, dumbfounded. "What do you mean, *lost* one?"

Another tech said, "Confirm that Bird Three is down, sir."

Storm Shadow was smiling, arms folded. "And so it begins."

McCullen said to him, irritably, "What?"

"We are under attack."

"Alert all defenses!" McCullen snapped. Then to Storm Shadow, he said, "What are you *smiling* about?"

"He's here," Storm Shadow said, but he wasn't really answering McCullen; the words were for himself.

His brother was here. . . .

Storm Shadow exited the control room, and when McCullen turned to say something to Ana, she was gone, too.

Above, on ground level, the G.I. JOE team watched the two surviving drones racing away.

Breaker asked, "What about those two?"

Scarlett was shaking her head. "They're already way out of range."

Rip said, "We better find their damn kill switches, then, or there'll be hell to pay."

Scarlett said, "We can't count on finding the kill switches. We need another option."

Breaker had one. "Somebody has to go up there and shoot those things down."

Rip drew in a breath. "I guess that'd be me. . . . Wasn't that a jet I saw in there?"

They all looked at him as if he were a madman, and maybe he was; but he was a madman already heading back in that cave.

CHAPTER FIFTEEN

Blast from the Past

Midday in Washington, D.C., the White House glistened in picture-postcard perfection, with nothing to give away the crisis in full throttle within those walls, and in particular in the Oval Office.

The president's two young staffers burst into the office accompanied by a contingent of Secret Service.

At his desk, the president sat erect and asked with a calm that he hoped was the center of this storm, "Yes? What is it?"

The lead Secret Service agent said, "Sir, Stratcom's tracking three warheads, just launched off the polar ice cap."

The male staffer said, "One was downed immediately, which is a plus."

The female said, "But the other two are currently entering the upper atmosphere."

The president's eyebrows were up. "On their way where?"

The Secret Service lead man said, "One seems headed here, Mr. President."

"Here, as in America?"

"Here," the agent said, "as in Washington, D.C. Sir, we need to get you to the Bunker—*now*."

At the polar ice cap, in the underwater MARS Industries facility, Duke was still wide awake, strapped down on an operating table, waiting for God knew what procedure.

The Doctor in the bizarre black mask with silver tubing—a breathing apparatus of some kind, Duke figured—had been making preparations at a computer console, while the small robots stood at attention waiting for further orders.

Duke's eyes were narrowed, as if they could bring this strange figure into better focus. "Who *are* you?"

The Doctor looked up from the console. "The man who will change you forever . . . you, and the world."

What kind of megalomaniacal ranting was this?

And why was that voice, behind its raspiness anyway, so damn familiar?

"Who *are* you, I said!" Duke strained against the straps, trying to sit up, without success.

The Doctor came over and seemed to be smiling behind the weird breathing apparatus. "Don't you recognize me, Duke?"

And then the Doctor reached up and snatched off long hair that was actually a wig, discarding it somewhere, before unlatching and sliding off the mask and monocle that had covered so much of his face.

That face was scarred, badly scarred, from burns so horrible that plastic surgery had done it little good. How frustrating it must have been to the brilliant mind entrapped in this monstrous body to be helpless against something as fundamental and simple as his own appearance.

But that appearance, despite the burns, was more than just familiar to Duke.

He knew this man.

This was Ana's brother, Rex!

"My God," Duke said, not straining at the straps now, too stunned to do anything but gape. "Ana *buried* you. . . ."

"A moving ceremony, I'm sure," intoned the lipless mouth in the ghastly scarred visage.

"You son of a—"

"The three-volley salute. Boots on the ground. Folded flag in her arms. And Duke, is that any way to greet your old friend? Your comrade-in-arms?"

"My God, why?" Duke asked, shaking his head, truly dumbfounded. "Why didn't you let us know you'd survived? Why didn't you come back with us . . . ? Were you unconscious in the flaming ruins, or . . . ?"

Rex was having trouble breathing now, and he returned his mask to his face. The rasp had returned to his voice when he said, "I could not return with you because I had discovered something."

"Something . . . on the mission, in that lab?"

He nodded, and his eyes seemed to go somewhere else, perhaps to that village and the laboratory he had entered while the insertion team led by Duke and Rip lay down cover from outside.

Duke had no way of knowing that the creature who had once been Rex was hearing a voice in his mind, the voice of an elderly man relating an audio diary of experiments.

And Rex could see, in his memory, what he'd beheld when he entered that jungle-encroached laboratory: images on monitors of men who had been victims of unsuccessful experiments, terrible images, worse even than his own scars. . . .

"The man who created this nanotechnology," Rex said from behind the mask, "was not our enemy. In fact, he was hired by our own government to research and create this weapon. Then, when other voices deemed his discoveries too unethical even for modern warfare, a team was sent in to kill him."

"Our insertion team," Duke said.

"Yes. Those were my top-secret orders, Duke— to retrieve as much of his research materials as possible, but . . . also to terminate the old man."

"*Did* you?"

"He asked me, when I entered his little jungle domain, if that was why I was there—'Are you going to shoot me?' I just told him to stay where he was, because already I knew I'd been lied to. The images on the computers were not what I'd been expecting, not chemical or nuclear . . . but, as the old man said, 'Something much better.' "

"Better," Duke said.

"I told him that what I was seeing was beyond anything I could have imagined . . . light-years ahead of anything developed by anyone in the research field. And he *knew* that—he said, 'It's going to change the world as we know it.' "

"What did you do?"

"I didn't kill him. Instead, I jammed a flash drive into the mainframe and started downloading the files. Then I heard the jets coming—early. Why did you have them come so soon? You ruined *everything*!"

"Somebody jumped the gun," Duke said.

"The old scientist had a vault big enough for us to seal ourselves in. He went in first, saying he would show me everything, if we survived. I could hear a bunker buster whistling toward us! Then the download finished, and I grabbed it and ran for the vault . . . but the door was closed."

"Yet you survived the blast."

"Yes. I lived, somewhat the worse for wear." He touched his face near the mask. "And escaped with my benefactor's research, which I have perfected over these four years. And now? Now you will get a firsthand demonstration."

Duke shook his head. "Does *Ana* know, Rex? Does she know about all this . . . about *you*?"

"No," he said quietly. "And she never will."

Again Rex stepped behind the main computer

console, and the Smart Robots came to life, and began moving menacingly in on the strapped-down patient.

In the ice cave, Ripcord had climbed up into the cockpit of the low-slung Night Raven jet, while Scarlett was right there next to him beside the sleek craft, keeping a concerned, mildly skeptical watch. The control panel came alive in front of him, and futuristic flight goggles wrapped themselves around his head.

"Now, y'see?" Rip said. "This is very cool. Gotta give the bad guys that much."

"How do you know you can even fly this thing?"

He smiled. "I can fly anything, from a kite to a rocket ship. You just find a way to guide me to those warheads."

"Right," she said. "Ripcord?"

"Yeah?"

She leaned forward and pressed her lips to his. Tenderly.

"Good luck," she said.

He gave her a warm look. "I'll be fine. Nobody ever had a sweeter send-off. But you do me a favor, okay?"

"Anything."

"Save Duke."

She gave him a crisp nod, and backed off, rejoining the rest of the team, while Rip quietly grinned to himself.

Soon the Night Raven was tearing across the ice

to launch itself skyward while Rip whooped in an adrenaline rush.

He had no way of knowing that in the Control Room of the Pit, where the two warheads were on one screen and the Night Raven on another, General Hawk was wide-eyed, yelling, "Ripcord? They let *Ripcord* fly that plane . . . God help us."

Meanwhile, Scarlett, Snake Eyes, and Breaker were fast-roping down the nearby launch bay from which the first drone had emerged. As they went, the ice reformed around them, as if the hole had never been there.

In the operating room below, a small robot was making an incision behind Duke's right ear.

And Duke could feel it—his old friend Rex's bedside manner did not include providing anesthetics to his grimacing patient.

Then a long needle zeroed in on that incision, and Duke was saying a silent prayer that included good-byes to family and friends, Rip included, when from behind he heard a *thud*.

A hand hit a switch, and the needle quickly retracted into the now frozen robot's grasp. Craning, Duke could see someone in black combat attire at the controls—*Ana*!

She was looking right at him now, after having knocked down a man she knew only as the Doctor with no notion that the fiend now stirring groggily at her feet was her "dead" brother, Rex.

"We don't have much time," she said.

She rushed to the operating table, untied Duke, and he was on his feet and the two one-time lovers stared at each other for a long moment.

Finally they kissed passionately, Duke's hand behind her head with his fingers buried in her sweet hair . . .

. . . *only he felt something there.*

An incision.

Their lips parted, their eyes still locked.

"Oh my God," he said. "What have they *done* to you?"

That was when Ana's body snapped rigid, then fell limp in his arms, her eyes wide open and staring with a terrible blankness.

"*Ana!*" Duke said.

His eyes went over to where the Doctor was pulling himself up on a panel of the console, and in one hand was a PDA, from which he had undoubtedly sent the order that "switched off" Ana.

Two Neo-Vipers strode in, pulse rifles aimed Duke's way, McCullen following, wearing a smile so smug his own mother would have wanted to wipe it off his face.

Duke was busy staring at the woman he loved, and desperately trying to find a pulse in her wrist.

In the flame-scorched vertical tunnel that was the launch bay, Scarlett, Snake Eyes and Breaker rappelled down to where the tube widened to reveal a chrome corridor beneath them yawning in either direction.

But they did not drop onto the shining surface. Snake Eyes touched something and his visor turned a darker black, while Breaker gestured down toward the chrome floor. An ominous electrical hum was in all of their ears.

"That surface down there," Breaker said, "is pressure-plated and laser-protected."

Scarlett, dangling on her rope, nodded. "Anything larger than a quarter that touches that floor is gonna get fried. . . ."

She and Breaker both turned to Snake Eyes.

He sighed heavily.

Ninja's work was never done. . . .

Duke stood holding the unconscious Ana tight, but his eyes were on Rex now. "You would do this to your own *sister*?"

The scarred, masked monster erupted in anger. "I *loved* my sister! Do you have any idea the state she was in—I was dead, you were AWOL, no good to her at all. I did her a favor."

"A *favor*?"

"Yes—I didn't want her to see me, to know me like this. Effectively, she had indeed lost me . . . and you. So I gave her a way to deal with her pain. And I gave her empty life a purpose."

Duke's eyes and nostrils flared like a rearing horse. "She wouldn't give a damn what you look like. You could have stopped her pain just by letting her know you were alive."

"Not without giving up my research," he said.

"She would never have understood . . . Anyway, science requires sacrifice. I am the living embodiment of that dictum, Duke."

"Every bad thing she's done," Duke said, "has been because of you. Because of your sick *tampering. . . .*"

The Doctor gestured with an upraised forefinger of a gloved hand.

"Not entirely because of me, Duke. There's you abandoning her—let's not forget about that."

That stung Duke, and he found he had nothing more to say to this monster.

McCullen stepped forward and said to the Doctor, "Is she alive?"

"For the present."

"I thought," McCullen said irritably, "we had complete control. You said this couldn't happen!"

The Doctor shrugged rather grandly. "I didn't think it possible. I've never seen anyone override the programming . . . not even momentarily."

Fury flushed McCullen's face, and he thrust a pointing finger at Duke as if aiming a weapon. "Do you mean, she was able to override it because of *him*?"

"Apparently," the Doctor said, as calm as if he were discussing the results of yet another experiment. "And the pain must have been *excruciating.*"

As Breaker and Scarlett hung on their ropes in the bay launch tube, Snake Eyes dropped to the laser-fortified floor of the chrome corridor below . . .

somersaulting in the air to land on the tips of his fingers.

Scarlett, watching, could only be amazed by the man's incredible dexterity and strength, as the ninja walked on his fingertips with the crackle and hum of lasers all around.

Still on his fingertips, Snake Eyes reached the silver panel of a doorway.

Breaker was calling out: "What you'll have to do is rewrite the laser panel's brain by—"

But Snake Eyes, balancing on the fingertips of one hand now, grabbed a sword from an over-the-shoulder sheath and stabbed the laser panel.

And the laser netting vanished, leaving only silence.

"Or," Breaker said, "you could just stab it."

Scarlett said into her headset, "We're in."

And back in the Control Room of the Pit, General Hawk ordered the deployment of the SHARCs—Submersible High-Speed Attack and Reconnaissance Crafts.

In the Arctic Ocean, the G.I. JOE submarine was hurtling toward the underwater MARS base, a shining metallic fortress that was clearly the work of a shipbuilder. As the sub approached its target, dozens of sleek, ivory-color G.I. JOE SHARCS peeled off the sides of the sub.

In the lead SHARC, Heavy Duty was driving, with a gunner behind him.

Back at the MARS facility, their own attack

vehicles—dozens of the sleekly finned, three-man mini-sub called Mantis—were being launched.

An epic conflagration was about to begin.

As the underwater base was rocked by fire from the SHARCS and the G.I. sub, the flight control room felt the impact, the techs rocked, while Mc-Cullen immediately hit a com switch.

"Fire up the pulse cannon!" he commanded.

The first blast of the turbo-pulse cannon destroyed three SHARCs, just missing Heavy Duty's, one of the crafts cartwheeling into the enemy base to explode, ripping apart a section of outer wall.

Heavy Duty said into his headset, "Everybody stay tight on the enemy craft! Don't let that cannon catch you out in the open!"

Scarlett, Breaker, and Snake Eyes charged into the enemy flight control room, cutting down technicians and Neo-Vipers in a fast, one-sided firefight, after which Scarlett sealed the doors while Breaker took over one of the computer stations.

"Ripcord," Breaker said into a mic, "can you hear me?"

Rip's voice came right back: *Loud and clear—what's the word?*

"I've got the coordinates of the other two warheads."

"Shoot. Pardon the expression."

"Target One is Moscow! Target Two is Washington, D.C."

In the cockpit of the Night Raven, Rip skimmed above the earth and said to his brand-new plane, "C'mon, Baby—time to show Daddy what you can do. . . ."

He jammed the throttle forward and the Night Raven jumped into even faster flight.

In Washington, D.C., in a corridor deep under the White House, the president's Secret Service bodyguards rushed him and his staff toward a fortified bunker.

He asked, "How soon will the warhead hit the city?"

"Seventeen minutes, sir."

"This will be a disaster the likes of which this nation has never seen. You've talked to my wife?"

"Yes—she and the rest of your family are in the Camp David bunker right now."

"Thank God." He shook his head, his expression grave.

"But so many others—so many families. . . . It's unimaginable."

The doors closed after them, as the group entered the bunker, whose doors bore the logo of MARS Industries, which had acquired the defense contract that included monitoring the president's safety in just such a situation.

The pulse cannon pivoted, locked onto the G.I. JOE submarine, and fired—taking the sub out in a massive explosion that mingled fire with a horrible bloody bubbling froth.

Heavy Duty said, "Bastards just blew up the sub!"

Back at the Pit, General Hawk had already seen as much, and he called out, "Somebody take out that damn *cannon*!"

In the enemy flight control room, where alarm lights were flashing and klaxons were crying, Scarlett responded to the general: "We're *on* it, sir!"

She got a map of the facility onto a screen and showed it to Snake Eyes, saying, "The cannon control room should be up in this silo, right here . . . where all the laser conduits converge. Okay?"

Snake Eyes nodded, and ran out of the control room.

Never have to tell him twice, Scarlett thought.

In the Night Raven, Rip was streaking into the upper atmosphere, the curve of the earth visible out his cockpit windows. Then, up ahead, he could make out the pulsating green light of the warhead in flight.

"I can see it," Rip said into his headset. "Dead ahead."

In the enemy control room, Breaker said, *"Rip, you have to knock it down before it reenters the atmosphere."*

Scarlett said, *"If those nano-mites hit the ground, it's all over. . . ."*

Rip flicked a switch on his instrument panel and opened a pulse laser on the jet's nose.

"Uh, Houston, we have a problem," Rip said. "The firing controls are *not* in here."

Breaker's voice in his ear said: *"What do you mean, 'not in there'?"*

"That was English! I mean, I can't see 'em *anywhere*!"

In the operating room, the impact of another explosion rattled everyone and everything, but it did provide Duke with a moment to grab one of Ana's pistols from her low-slung holsters, and kill the two skull-helmeted guards before he turned the gun on McCullen and the Doctor.

The Doctor lifted his PDA and his finger hovered over the "TERMINATE" button. "If I press this, Ana dies."

Tightly Duke said, "Put it down, Rex."

McCullen glanced at first one man and then the other, realizing for the first time that the two knew each other from another lifetime.

"It's your choice, Duke. . . ."

"But she's your *sister*. . . ."

Ana's eyes blinked—something was registering.

Back in the enemy flight control room, Scarlett had a thought. "It must be voice-activated!"

In her ear, Rip's voice said: *"What?"*

"It's an audible command—you have to speak the words into your flight helmet."

In the Night Raven, Rip said, "Roger that," and lined up the missile in his sights.

Got a lock. . . .

"Fire!" he said.

Nothing.

"Shoot!"

Nothing.

"Blast away!"

Still nothing.

The missile was streaking onward toward its earthbound target.

"Nothing's happening," Rip said.

Scarlett's voice: *"It must be a different language. Try 'teine.' "*

"Say what?"

"It's Celt—Scottish, like McCullen is Scottish—for 'fire.' "

"Teine," Rip tried, but his version sounded about as Scottish as chow mein.

"You've got to get a Scottish lilt into it—listen to my voice: 'Teine!' "

"Teine, teine, teine," Rip said, still not catching the melody Scarlett had been singing. "It's not working!"

"That's because you're not saying it right."

"How many different ways you want me to say it, girl?"

"One way—the right way! Teine!"

Rip tried again, and this time the lilt was there: "Teine!"

And at last the pulse laser fired, blasting the missile out of the sky, a greenish cloud of nano-mites floating aimlessly away.

In the enemy flight control room, the missile had disappeared on the screen, getting big smiles out of both Scarlett and Breaker.

"Nice work, Ace," she told Rip. You just saved Moscow!"

In the cockpit of the Night Raven, Rip sighed relief, already peeling away.

"Just doin' my job," he said. "Now guide me to that other drone."

And in his mind, where he was doing cartwheels, Rip thought, *Man, I just saved freakin' Moscow!*

CHAPTER SIXTEEN

In the operating chamber, Duke had Ana's pulse pistol trained on the Doctor, whose fingers hovered over his PDA. To one side, McCullen was watching this standoff, discreetly reaching for a high-tech blowtorch.

Even so, the CEO could not resist taunting Duke: "Did you think she loved *you*? Did you imagine your life would be with her?" McCullen's laugh was sandpaper harsh. "Don't you know she was *never* yours?"

Duke, looking from Rex to McCullen, said, "All I know is, neither one of you bastards is worthy of her."

Rex's eyes flared over the breathing mask. "And you *are,* you cretinous, musclebound fool?"

With Duke's attention back on the Doctor, Mc-Cullen made his move, lifting the blowtorch and shooting an orange-and-blue tongue flame Duke's way.

But the fighting man's reflexes saved him, as he pivoted and fired Ana's pistol, hitting not Mc-

Cullen but one of the robots, blowing the flames and the robot back at the CEO in a burst that sent both man and metal-bot through the door and out into the corridor.

The Doctor took some force from the blast, as well, and was blown to the floor, losing his PDA in the process; but he didn't take time to try to recover it, instead scrambling out into the corridor, where McCullen and the flames had gone, along with the rubble that had been a robot.

Duke quickly snatched up the PDA, removed Ana's screen with its "TERMINATE" button unpressed, and breathed in air that tasted scorched, from the blowtorch's aftermath.

In the corridor, a screaming McCullen, his face and hands and suit aflame, rolled on the floor, trying to put the fire out.

He'd just about accomplished that when the Doctor came along, grabbed onto an arm and pulled the man to his feet to drag him down the corridor. McCullen screamed in agony all the way, his face and hands a terrible bright pink touched here and there with crispy black.

The president's book-lined office in the bunker had become a sort of war room, with a Secret Service agent on a secure line right now.

The agent paused to look at the President—seated behind a smaller desk than his Oval Office one—to say, "The warhead heading for Moscow? One of the JOEs just shot it down."

"Thank God. But Washington is still at risk?"

"That missile is in play, Mr. President, yes."

The leader of the free world shook his head glumly. *Could this day be more of a nightmare?* he wondered.

The answer was yes, because at that moment another Secret Service agent drew a silenced automatic and systematically shot the agent who'd been on the phone and every other agent and White House staff member present, like a housekeeper making sure every object on a mantle had been dusted, sparing only the president himself.

The president, in his horror, nonetheless noticed something odd about the agent—if killing everyone present but the president himself hadn't been odd enough—and that was a distinctive incision scar behind the man's right ear. The significance of this was lost on the president, but this was indeed a Neo-Viper who had been undercover.

Then a bookcase wall slid open, revealing a secret chamber and a figure who was just about to step out of the shadows.

"My God," the president said.

What horror awaited him next?

As the underwater battle raged, torpedoes plastered the enemy base, but the G.I. JOEs took their share of hits. A gunner in the SHARC next to Heavy Duty was blown right out of his craft by one of those mini-subs.

Heavy D angled his SHARC to collide with the

mini-sub's bubble top and smashed the thing, sending the craft careening, its driver dead or soon to be.

Into his headset, Heavy Duty said, "We need that pulse cannon knocked out! It's *killing* us. How's it coming?"

Within the enemy base, the man to whom Heavy D's question was most pointedly asked did not reply, because Snake Eyes was not just a man of few words, he was a man of no words.

But also a man of action.

Right now the ninja in black was charging through a corridor toward a door. At the far end of that same corridor, unseen by Snake Eyes, another ninja—this one in white—rounded a corridor and caught a glimpse of Snake Eyes going through that door.

Storm Shadow—his tattered white business suit exchanged for his formal ninja attire, swords and all—picked up the pace, moving with renewed purpose.

In the turbo-cannon control room, technicians were manning the controls of the great weapon, a Neo-Viper standing guard. The techs were taken out with swift martial arts blows, and hadn't even seen Snake Eyes coming, while the Neo-Viper earned a kick that sent him flying through a glass window in a shower of shards down into the circular shaft around the pulse laser, traveling past a grated floor into the deadly freezing waters below.

Swiftly, Snake Eyes took in the console's controls

and shut down the cannon, which could change the course of the battle.

Then he heard movement behind him, barely perceptible over the mechanical and electrical hum, and spun in time to take the shooting star in his shoulder and not somewhere vital.

The ninja in black yanked the sharp-edged star out and hurled it back at its owner, who deftly ducked it, then moved to take on his brother.

The ninjas moved in and around the claustrophobic control room, engaged in brutal hand-to-hand combat. As the two men fought in a dizzying display of marital-arts one-upmanship, a pair of techs rushed in and powered the pulse cannon back up.

Snake Eyes headed for that console, but Storm Shadow lunged at him, sending both of them flying out the already-broken window that had been "opened" by the Neo-Viper that Snakes Eyes had recently dispatched.

They tumbled past the central, glowing shaft onto the metal gridwork of the gangway halfway down, designed for service purposes.

As the two ninjas got to their feet, ten energy-source laser beams powered on between circuit modules on the wall, and in the central power shaft, as well. One of these beams caught Storm Shadow in the shoulder, and gave him a severe burn.

But the white-clad ninja overrode the pain, shook it off, and stood defiantly ready to continue battle with his childhood rival.

From somewhere, a Neo-Viper charged Snake Eyes, who almost casually kicked the skull-head into one of the laser beams, which killed him as quickly as a fly flying into a bug zapper.

Back online, the pulse cannon fired, and the lasers faded, as the effort soaked up their energy.

Storm Shadow drew his sword.

So did Snake Eyes.

The Doctor was half-dragging McCullen, who was struggling to stay on his feet, into the docking base even as the world exploded around them. Up ahead was the Trident submarine, waiting for them, two Neo-Vipers standing guard.

Within moments, with blasts going off seemingly just above them, the Doctor was helping McCullen down into the sub, the CEO's eyes wild in the horrifically burned red-and-black mask of his face.

As the sub's pilots were guiding it out of dock, the Doctor led his patient to a cabin and into a comfortable chair.

McCullen wasn't screaming now, shock setting in. Soon Rex had a syringe of glowing-green nanomite solution ready.

"This will only hurt a little," Rex said.

He began injecting the CEO behind the right ear.

"Later," Rex admitted, "more so. . . ."

And indeed McCullen was screaming even louder than before as the Trident began to submerge.

*   *   *

Elsewhere in the undersea MARS HQ, with water and fire blasting out behind and in front of him, Duke ran down a tubular corridor washed in blue light with a barely conscious Ana in his arms, a husband hurriedly carrying his bride across an endless threshold. He had her pulse pistol in one hand, and she cradled her brother's PDA in her lap.

Charging into the underwater base's docking bay, still with Ana in his arms, Duke saw the sub submerging, as well as a trio of pilots getting ready to get into Mantis mini-subs. Duke set Ana down, and her PDA tumbled to the dock, making a *clunk,* and the three sub pilots turned their way.

Duke triggered the pulse pistol and sent their crushed remains flying.

Ana, prone on the dock, was looking up at him, tears in her eyes. "Duke . . . ?"

He knelt by her.

"That hideous doctor . . . that was *Rex,* wasn't it?"

He could only nod.

Her face hardened, her eyes traveling to the PDA she'd dropped. She grabbed it up into her grasp.

"He betrayed me," she said bitterly. "They all betrayed me . . . lied to me . . . manipulated me . . . even you, Duke. . . ."

"Ana, there'll be time for that later. I have to get you out of here—now."

He helped her to her feet and they hobbled toward a Mantis mini-sub at the docking area.

* * *

In the enemy flight control room, Scarlett and Breaker were hunkered at a computer console while a shower of sparks began to spurt from a sealed door, promising an invasion of God knew how many of those skull-helmeted adversaries.

"We're running out of time," Scarlett said.

Breaker pointed at one of the security-cam screens. "Look! It's Duke!"

"And . . . the *Baroness*?"

Breaker shrugged. "He looks all right—she looks worse off than he does."

"But what is he *doing* with her?"

The door exploded open and half a dozen of the skull-heads rushed in, firing willy-nilly as they advanced, blasting glass, monitors, and computers.

Scarlett returned fire, killing two before a swipe from a passing pulse pistol blast took her off her feet and deposited her rudely on the floor, air knocked out of her. The remaining trio of Neo-Vipers got the drop on her, while Breaker threw his hands up in surrender.

Scarlett got to her feet and her eyes met Breaker's—they were going to be executed. Simple as that. They exchanged a curt comradely nod.

An honor serving with you. . . .

Then two of the enemies dropped to the floor. Limp as puppets with their strings snipped, and deader than hell.

The remaining one, startled by the sight, gave Scarlett the opportunity to send an arrow straight through his eye-slit, killing him, too.

Now the two JOEs exchanged little relieved grins—neither had any idea why they were still alive.

Within the mini-sub, Duke was in front, Ana in back, scrolling with seething determination through screen after screen of Neo-Vipers, hitting their TERMINATE buttons before moving to the next. This had been the action that had saved Scarlett and Breaker.

Duke was submerging the Mantis. "Fire up your harpoon cannon, Ana! We have work to do."

"I'm already at work," she said, "letting my darling brother know that I am still alive. . . ."

All around the base, Neo-Vipers on the run down corridors, standing guard at various posts, began collapsing, one at a time, landing in sprawling, lifeless heaps.

And among the Neo-Vipers she terminated was one designated: SECRET SERVICE NEO-VIPER.

Which was why the Neo-Viper posing as a Secret Service agent, in the president's bunker, keeled over and expired like a parking meter, sending the astonished and very much relieved leader of the free world to his feet behind his desk.

In the enemy flight control room, Breaker—leaping back to his console, which mercifully hadn't taken any hits from the brief Neo-Viper invasion—had figured it out.

"Somebody's killing those super soldiers remotely," he told Scarlett. "Shutting off their switches. Lights out."

"You stay on the horn with Ripcord," she said. "I'm going to find Duke."

At another console, she began searching through the seemingly countless security-cam screens. Finally she located Duke and Ana in their Mantis. He had a helmet on that went with the craft, and allowed Scarlett, through her console, to contact him.

"Hey, Duke—it's Scarlett. How you doing?"

"Hey, Scarlett—good to hear your voice. But I've had better days."

"You and me both. What are you up to? Figure it's a nice morning for an outing?"

"Oh yeah—I'm going after McCullen. And, trust me, you guys need to get the hell out of there."

"Can't just yet," she said. "Rip's gotta take out one more nano-mite warhead, and I'm his eyes and ears."

"Rip? Where is he, anyway?"

"Long story, Duke. Don't ask. But you can say hello, if you want."

She threw a switch.

Tentatively, Duke said, "Hello?"

Rip's voice came into Duke's helmet-com. *"Duke! You are alive!"*

"Seem to be. So, uh, how's it going?"

Up in the Night Raven, Rip was smiling through a face full of sweat and a body riddled with adrenaline. "Livin' a brother's dream, my man! Livin' a brother's dream. . . ."

In the enemy control room, Breaker and Scarlett had Rip on their screens.

Breaker said, "Hurry, Rip! You've only got thirty seconds before that nano-mite warhead enters the lower atmosphere."

Up in his jet, Rip was feeling the pressure. But he had the missile in his sights.

"Taine!" he said.

In his ear, Scarlett's voice corrected him: *"Teine! Teine!"*

"Don't yell at me!" Rip said. "I told you, I'm sensitive."

Almost tenderly, her voice came: *"Teine."*

Ripcord took a deep breath, stealing his nerves, just as a red fuel light began beeping on his control panel. This he did his best to ignore, focusing on the missile as it receded into the lower atmosphere.

"Teine!" Rip said, spot-on in his enunciation.

The laser pulse fired, blasting straight at the missile, which was now lost in the atmospheric haze below.

Nothing.

Nothing, anyway, except the annoyingly persistent beep of that fuel lamp.

Scarlett's voice in his ear delivered the bad news: *"You missed!"*

Breaker's voice came: *"The warhead has entered the lower atmosphere!"*

Soon, so had Rip and the Night Raven.

And below them spread out the vista of Washington, D.C.

Duke's mini-sub rocketed up out of a port in the ground-level ice tunnel.

He had discovered the mini-sub, which Ana called a Mantis, had dry-land capability, like the GI JOE crafts called SHARCs—in fact, like the SHARCs the things could fly, and the controls were such that he thought he could handle it.

Certainly the pilots of three other of the Mantis crafts could handle their controls, because the buglike buggies were swarming toward his mantis in the big open ice cavern.

"*Shoot* those guys!" Duke told Ana.

Ana was on a harpoon cannon, but a SHARC had come into view and she automatically, reflexively, blew it to hell.

"Not *those* guys," Duke told her.

He pointed.

"*Those* guys, Ana—the ones trying to *kill* us?"

He could sense her reluctance, as she lined her cannon up on the Mantis pursuing Duke's craft down an ice tunnel.

Snake Eyes slid under a laser beam and slashed Storm Shadow's leg, then did a run up the wall, to evade his brother's blades. The black-clad ninja did get cut when he came back down, but he returned the favor, slicing the white-clad ninja across the stomach, shredding his jacket.

Storm Shadow responded with a deft series of blows that took the sword right out of the other ninja's grasp, then finished with a slashing blow across the face, which was absorbed by Snake Eye's mask.

Still, Snake Eyes had been staggered by the blow, and Storm Shadow might have finished him, if the mighty pulse cannon hadn't fired up again at that very moment, sending a laser beam burning into Storm Shadow's jacket.

Quickly Storm Shadow used his blade to deflect the laser, reflecting it back at Snake Eyes, who flipped and landed, with the laser touching barely an inch below his groin.

Under his hood, Storm Shadow grinned.

Then he stuck his swords into the grating, and peeled off his hood and jacket, just as Snake Eyes got back to his feet.

Storm Shadow said, in Japanese, *"You took a vow of silence. . . . Now you will die without a word."*

The bare-chested ninja kicked his brother's fallen sword toward him, but Snake instead drew a pair of tonfas, side-handled batons.

Storm Shadow's grin faded as he moved into position and the two ninjas went at each other yet again.

Ripcord was gunning the Night Raven after the missile, chasing it down the Potomac, ripping up river water in huge sprays, getting real close this time . . . *no way he was gonna miss again. . . .*

But a voice in his ear, Breaker's, said, *"You're too close, Rip—back off. You don't have to be this close."*

But Rip was in the zone, feeling an almost eerie sense of calm. "Actually, Breaker boy, I think I'm just about close enough . . . *teine.*"

The pulse laser fired point blank, the missile exploding right in front of Rip, who was now flying through flames.

But a cloud of nano-mites was latching onto his wings.

CHAPTER SEVENTEEN

Face of a Cobra

In the enemy flight control room of the underwater base, Scarlett leaned toward the monitor to confirm her own eyes: the missile had disappeared from their screens.

But so had Ripcord. . . .

She spoke urgently into her mic: "Rip. . . . *Rip!*"

In the Night Raven, which shimmied at low altitude over Washington, D.C., Rip was struggling mightily with the controls as nano-mites swiftly gobbled up the metal of his craft even as his fuel light flashed at him tauntingly.

As he angled the jet upward, the silvery shimmer of the nano-mites was everywhere. . . .

Many miles away, Scarlett and Breaker were relieved to see the plane climbing.

She said, "He's taking the nano-mites back into the upper atmosphere—where they can't survive!"

"Go, Rip," Breaker breathed. *"Go. . . ."*

In the winding, ice-walled tunnel, Duke at the

helm of the flying Mantis was dodging the torpedoes that were exploding all around him.

But his mind was on his pal, and he, too, said, "Ripcord! *Go,* buddy!"

And the jet was in the upper atmosphere now, the nano-mites dying, withering, dropping away; but at the same time, the Night Raven had suffered so much structural damage, it was breaking up all around Rip. . . .

In the flight control room, Scarlett seemed to be trying to climb inside the monitor. "Eject, Rip! *Eject!*"

"*How?*" came Rip's voice.

Breaker said to Scarlett, "He'll need a code. What's Celt for eject, anyway?"

Scarlett said, "*Cur magh,* Rip! That's the command! *Cur magh!*"

Ripcord turned the jet over, flying upside down as he gave the command: "*Cur magh!*"

This time, it only took one try, as immediately the jet's canopy exploded off, sending Rip into the raging winds.

On her flight control room monitor, Scarlett could see that her command had worked, and so could Breaker, who said in a hushed, amazed voice, "He did it . . . he actually *did* it. . . ."

In her mic, Scarlett said, "Ripcord? *Talk* to me . . ."

But there was only silence broken lightly by faint static over the radio, and Scarlett and Breaker exchanged grim expressions.

Then Scarlett said, "Ripcord! *Ripcord!* Damn it, are you *there*?"

"*I told you, girl,*" Rip's voice came, "*not to yell at me. Here you go again, getting all emotional on me.*"

Scarlett's smile was immediate, relief rushing through both the JOEs in the enemy flight control room, Breaker saying into his mic, "Rip, man—are you okay?"

"*Yeah, bro. Did it work? Is D.C. in one piece?*"

"Yes," Scarlett said. "Yes, it worked. You saved the day."

In the sky over the nation's capital, Ripcord was floating down with a big, wide grin that threatened to blot out the morning sun.

"*Good to hear. Good to hear . . . 'cause, uh . . . uh oh. . . .*"

In the flight control room, Scarlett said, "What do you mean, 'uh oh'?"

Heavy fabric rustling followed by a heavy *thump* came over Rip's line, and had Scarlett and Breaker trading worried looks again.

But then Rip's voice was there: "*I was sayin' . . . that's good to hear, 'cause I could use gettin' cut a little slack about now.*"

Scarlett asked, "How's that?"

"*I, uh . . . think I'm about to get* arrested *again. . . .*"

The two JOEs in the underwater base flight control room had no idea what Rip was talking about—that in fact the team's newest favorite pilot had landed on the White House lawn, and was currently holding his hands up and smiling feebly as dozens of Secret Service Agents closed in around him.

In an ice tunnel, pursued by bad guys, Duke at the controls of a Mantis had been listening in on all of this, and despite his situation, he was smiling.

"The man did tell me he was jet qualified," Duke said.

In the pulse cannon's energy shaft, on the metal-grid gangway, the two ninjas continued their epic duel, both exhausted and wounded now, their perfect uniforms no longer very perfect at all, torn, bloodied, soiled.

Right now, using his tonfas, Snake Eyes was hammering back Storm Shadow, who was smiling, impressed.

But Storm Shadow's smile vanished when Snake Eyes triggered a pair of blades that popped out of either end of the tonfas with a *shick*!

The bare-chested ninja spun and, in the process, locked his two swords together, creating an extended blade.

This Snake Eyes blocked with his tonfas, as the energy lasers kicked back on and, in and around exchanging blows, the two had to use their weapons to bat the laser bursts away, often at each other.

As they fought at the edge of the gangway, one such beam caught Storm Shadow, and Snake Eyes took advantage of his opponent's slight hesitation to stab him in the chest with a tonfa blade . . .

. . . a potentially mortal blow that seemed to end the match here.

And both men knew that.

Their eyes met, and locked.

"One thing you must know," Storm Shadow said. "I did *not* kill our master. . . ."

As if to say, *And you should know—I don't believe you,* Snake Eyes lunged.

But Storm Shadow tumbled off the gangway, perhaps as a defensive move, or maybe just unconscious from the terrible wound Snake Eyes had inflicted; in any event, the ninja went limply down into the freezing waters below, with a splash that came up to fleck the other ninja's visor.

Snake Eyes stood there watching for an eternity that was perhaps a full minute.

But Storm Shadow never surfaced.

Then Heavy Duty's voice came into the ninja's ear: *"Snake Eyes! They got a* lock *on me!"*

Indeed, the laser was pulsing, full force, getting ready to power up another turbo-cannon blast.

Snake Eyes spun and threw his tonfas up at a control panel where technicians were back at their post, only now to fall dead, each getting a blade.

Once the pulse cannon was disabled, Snake Eyes ran out of the energy shaft, typing a quick text message on his wrist-communicator.

In the seat of his SHARC, brow beaded with sweat, Heavy Duty saw the message on his control panel screen: "CANNON OFF-LINE. HAVE A NICE DAY."

Heavy D grinned. "I don't care what anybody says. The boy has a sense of humor."

In the labyrinthian ice tunnel, Duke and Ana had two Mantis crafts on their tail, blasting away at them.

Duke rocketed around a corner just in time to see a big Trident submarine disappearing behind a huge steel port, which was spiraling swiftly shut.

"Oh, no no no *no,* you don't!" Duke said, and fired off two torpedoes that raced toward the submarine . . .

. . . but impacted only on the now shut port.

"Damn it!" Duke said, over the blast.

Behind him, Ana said, "Uh, Duke. . . ."

They were heading right toward that same metal port right now, and the two Mantises were charging up behind them.

"Oh, damn," Duke said.

"*Duke!*" Ana said.

On that fleeing submarine, Ana's brother, the Doctor, was giving instructions to a pair of Neo-Vipers: "Detonate the ice pack."

Duke yanked back on the stick and flipped upright and over the first Mantis, which flew straight under him and smashed like a bug into a windshield against the huge metallic closed door, making a bright blossom of flame.

Then Duke fired a pair of torpedoes point blank at the second Mantis, blowing it to pieces.

That got a victory *whoop* out of Duke, cut short when Ana said, "I've got orders on a screen back here—they're telling the other Mantis crafts to abort! . . . Good God, that means they're going to blow the ice pack. . . ."

Immediately Duke gunned his craft and, on every channel available to him, called out the warning: *"This is Duke calling all JOEs! The ice pack is coming down, repeat, the ice pack is coming down! Get the hell out!"*

In his SHARC, Heavy Duty gave the ice pack above him an ominous frown, and then spread the word: *"Everybody pull back! Pull out now!"*

All of the remaining SHARCs started making a fast retreat from the base as a string of detonations exploded deep inside the cliffs of ice.

In the flight control room, hell had already broken loose, Scarlett yanking Breaker out as the room imploded under a foaming gush of freezing water.

Soon the pair was charging through corridors as the base exploded around them, icy water and leaping flames peacefully coexisting to create horrific obstacles for escape.

In the ice tunnel above, Duke and Ana in their Mantis were barely clearing the fire and ice exploding all around them.

"Cutting it close, Duke," she pointed out.

"You think?"

For what it was worth, back at the Control Room of the Pit, General Hawk's eyes were traveling from screen to screen, as if following a hellish sporting event, cheering his people on: "C'mon, guys . . . get outa there . . . get *outa* there. . . ."

And at the underwater base, Scarlett and Breaker had made it to the diving bell entry port. They looked around frantically and were rewarded with the sight of a battle-weary Snake Eyes, staggering up.

Scarlett ran to him and embraced him. "Snake, thank God. . . . We don't have much time. . . ."

A nearby explosion underscored this, sending them dashing toward the diving bell. Snake Eyes shook off the pain and kept pace, and in moments they were within the diving bell. Breaker quickly got the doors closed, and the bell launched.

Duke and Ana in their Mantis rocketed out of the imploding ice tunnel while, behind them, the ice pack was sheeting down onto the underwater base, barely missing the retreating SHARCs.

Then a massive explosion—that made all that had preceded seem like so many firecrackers—took what remained of the base off its perch and over a cliff of ice into a watery abyss.

In his SHARC, Heavy Duty risked being turned to a pillar of salt to look back at where the evil city had been, worried, wondering how many of his comrades had gone down with the enemy's ship.

Then Scarlett's voice came into his ear: *"We are all clear. Repeat, we are* all *clear!"*

The strong-jawed, stoic Heavy D grinned like a kid starting summer vacation. He had a message to share, too: "Go, JOE!"

And cheers and whoops were exchanged all around, including back at the Control Room of the Pit, where even the general allowed himself a slight smile.

Very quietly, he echoed Heavy Duty's sentiment: "Go, JOEs."

In their Mantis, Duke looked back at Ana and smiled.

But she did not return it.

Her expression was blank, but there was something tragic in her tone: "What did someone say once? Always and forever . . . maybe not. Maybe we both lose."

He turned back, his smile ebbing.

Then he stared up at the shattered ice pack and understood what she was saying.

McCullen and Rex had escaped, and they controlled her in a manner with which Duke's mere love could not hope to compete.

In the MARS Industries submarine, long past any threat, the Doctor and his patient were in what had been the latter's cabin—quarters that would henceforth belong to the former.

McCullen sat in a comfortable chair and no longer was screaming—in fact, he showed no discomfort at all, although he may well have felt some. But who could know, with that perfectly-fitting silver mask of nano-mites covering his face?

The Doctor, from deep in the room, said, "Nano-mites—my perfect little healers."

McCullen caught his reflection in a window and his fingers clawed at the mask, but the nano-mites twisted with the contours of his muscles to reveal, to his complete and ever-lasting horror, that the mask they'd formed was permanent.

Breaking down, he tumbled from the chair to the floor, distraught, his agony emotional now. "I have finally . . . finally taken my place in the long line of McCullens . . . *another* masked prisoner."

"You are not my prisoner. You are my servant, but do not despair. Every great man needs a second-in-command, and you shall be mine."

". . . Yours?"

"Yes. You see, James McCullen is no more. Now? Now we will indeed honor your fabled ancestor. Now you are *Destro*."

McCullen got to his feet and lunged toward the Doctor, saying, "What have you *done* to me, you fiend!"

The Doctor's finger touched a button on a new, smaller PDA and instantly McCullen stopped, frozen a few feet away and, once again, screaming in extreme pain as electric currents made a rippling wreath about his head.

Again, McCullen—Destro—fell to the floor of the cabin and began whimpering like a wounded pup.

With his back to his fallen subordinate, the Doctor affixed a new mask to himself, a much-improved and more stylish version of the breathing apparatus that would also serve a secondary purpose of suggesting strength and even striking terror in those who served him . . . and those he sought to enslave. . . .

"After long taking comfort in the shadows," said the man who had once been Ana's brother Rex, "the time has come for the cobra to rise up and reveal himself."

McCullen looked up and saw the Doctor with the new and disturbing mask covering his scarred features—black and red and suggesting the head of a cobra, nature's perfect killing machine, as the Doctor had once called it.

But the Doctor was no more.

"You will call me," the man in the haunting red-and-black mask said, "Commander."

"Commander," Destro muttered.

"And we will call our organization . . . *Cobra*."

The Cobra Commander touched a button on the PDA and the submarine, racing into deep arctic waters, made its own cosmetic change—the MARS Industries logo on its side disappearing as panels moved along the stern to replace it with a new insigna.

The COBRA insignia.

CHAPTER EIGHTEEN
Yo JOE

In a top-secret maximum security prison, operated by the G.I. JOE team under the authorization of its international members, Duke Hauser and Lifeline, the top JOE medical officer, were looking through a two-way mirror into the holding cell where Ana was seated, alone, staring blankly at nothing at all.

The medic was shaking his head, saying, "I've never seen encoding the likes of this."

"What's her physical condition, doc?"

The bearded man shrugged. "Physically, she's fine. But whoever programmed those negative factors into her sure didn't want anybody else shutting them off. That she overrode them to the degree she did is a small miracle . . . and a testimony to how she felt about you."

"Felt . . . or feels?"

"Ask me something I'm qualified to answer."

Duke stared at the beautiful prisoner. "There's nothing you can do?"

"Only the doctor who put that programming in there can take it out."

Duke thought that over, carefully.

Then he said, "Then I know what I've got to do."

Lifeline sighed and said, "Good luck, son. I'll do whatever I can for both of you."

And he patted Duke on the shoulder, and started out of the room.

Duke turned just as the medic was halfway out. "I want to talk to her."

"I can make that happen."

Soon Duke was walking along a prison corridor with Ana, accompanied by two prison guards. She walked slowly, her hands and feet shackled.

"You're gonna be seeing a lot of me around here," he said.

She shook her head, the dark locks bouncing off her shoulders. "Duke, it's no use. You can't beat this."

"Ana, I'm not going away. *We're* going to beat this."

Her expression remained glum. "You can't save me, Duke. No one can. I'm not sure anyone *should,* not after all I've done. . . ."

"It wasn't the real you who did those things."

Her smile was tiny yet very bitter. "It was more me than you want to believe . . ." And to herself: "It felt good, when I was doing those bad things . . . that's the worst part."

They were at the door of her cell block.

He said, "I'll never give up on you. Never. Remember—now and forever."

She seemed about to give in, and let some emotion through, but then a smile cracked her lips, and something sinister was in it.

"You do *know*, don't you," she said, "that this is only the beginning?"

She touched the scar he'd earned in the jungle, trying to save Rex, and the sinister smile melted into something almost tender.

Then prison bars were slamming shut between them.

Looking through them, she held his eyes, until the two prison guards led her away, Duke watching her go, devastated.

Finally, nothing was left but for him to walk off. Alone.

Because the G.I. JOE base had been exposed to the enemy, a big move was under way to new, even more elaborate digs, at an as yet undisclosed location. The team had literally knocked down the nano-mite missile threat, leading to their reinstatement by every member government.

Right now, on the landing platform, packing and loading were well under way as a Howler transport waited.

General Hawk and Heavy Duty were escorting Duke and Ripcord toward the ship, where Scarlett,

Snake Eyes, and Breaker were already onboard, waiting.

"With G.I. JOE reinstated," the general was saying, "Heavy Duty here has recommended that you boys be taken off provisional status."

Duke twitched a smile. "Really? What exactly are you saying, General?"

General Hawk shrugged. "That Heavy Duty thinks you boys should stick around."

"But are *you* asking us?" Duke was openly grinning now. "Because as I understand it, *you* have to ask."

Rip was nodding. "Yeah, that didn't sound like you were asking us, General. I mean, Heavy Duty is cool, but he ain't in charge."

"And you have to get asked," Duke said, that brazen smile still shining, "to get into G.I. JOE, right?"

"All right," Hawk said, throwing the smile right back at Duke. "I'm asking."

"Then we're in," Rip said.

"And damn proud to be," Duke said.

They were at the Howler now. Rip noticed Scarlett eavesdropping on all of this, smiling, her red hair tumbling off her shoulders.

Rip asked her, "So how do *you* feel about this? Duke and me coming aboard?"

"How do I feel?"

"Yeah, girl. How do you *feel*. . . ."

She pretended to be thinking hard about that

question. Then she said, innocently, "I feel very . . . emotional."

That got big laughs out of everyone, and the platform began to rise.

From the Howler, Heavy Duty and Breaker said, *"Yo JOE!"*

And everybody echoed that.

They allowed themselves these moments of comradery and even happiness, because they knew more battles lay ahead, with the threat of a new, even stronger foe rising out of the ashes of MARS Industries, an evil force that would soon be known to them as Cobra.

The fangs of this serpent had already spread their venom. Cobra had, after all, reached its influence into the Secret Service and the White House itself, although apparently that crisis was past, after the tragic incident in the presidential bunker.

Even now, a bevy of secretaries and staffers were greeting a much-refreshed, extremely confident president, on his way to the Oval Office, where he closed the door and enjoyed a few moments, alone.

He looked around, as if seeing these familiar quarters for the first time, and finally sat behind the fabled desk.

He cracked his knuckles.

He began whistling a jaunty tune.

Neither of these gestures, of course, were common to the president.

But they were habitual of a certain one-time aide of James McCullen of MARS Industries—a mimic called Zartan, who these days answered to a new master.

ALSO AVAILABLE FROM TITAN BOOKS:

THE RISE OF COBRA:
MISSION DOSSIER

G.I Joe: The Rise Of Cobra featuring the high-octane adventures of the original "action figure" team is the movie G.I Joe fans the world over have been waiting for. The G.I Joe: Mission Dossier unlocks the thrilling story of this brand-new all-action movie adventure.

This full colour companion to the movie features: interviews with the cast, full-colour stills, production art and weapon, vehicle and base schematics. Plus intel on all the G.I Joe team members and their enemies, as well as details on the amazing locations, the slick cutting-edge technology, and the fantastic stunts and special effects. It's a must for all G.I Joe fans!

WWW.TITANBOOKS.COM